A Waiting
Legacy

THE SEVENTH CHILD SERIES

JOY PENNOCK GAGE

A Land of Heart's Desire
Book 1

Lee William's Quest
Book 2

A Waiting Legacy
Book 3

A Waiting Legacy

Joy Pennock Gage

Harold Shaw Publishers
Wheaton, Illinois

ISBN 0-87788-850-7

Cover design by Ron Kadrmas

Cover illustration © 1991 by Kevin Beilfuss

Library of Congress Cataloging-in-Publication Data

Gage, Joy P.
    A waiting legacy / Joy Pennock Gage.
        p.   cm. — (The Seventh child series ; bk. 3)
    ISBN 0-87788-850-7
    I. Title. II. Series: Gage, Joy P. Seventh child series ; bk. 3.
    PS3557.A329W35   1991
8813'.54—dc20   91-8594
                                                        CIP

---

00 99 98 97 96 95 94 93 92 91
10 9 8 7 6 5 4 3 2 1

To
my father,
who is also the seventh child
of the seventh son
of the seventh child

CONTENTS

Acknowledgments

One does not attempt to write historical fiction without the proper resources. Much information is gained in bits and pieces—a date is verified, an interesting fact pointed out, a plant or night sound identified, a forgotten skill described. Such "trivia" joins together to recreate the daily lives of characters who inhabit the world of 150 years ago.

I wish to thank the following people who, each in their own way, have contributed significantly to the *Seventh Child Series:* The staff at Marin County (California) Civic Center Library; The Boston (Massachusetts) Public Library; The Missouri Historical Society, Columbia; Dr. Lee W. Toms for extensive use of his private library; Mr. and Mrs. Clay Baldwin; Mr. John Coons; Mrs. Carolyn Glass; Mr. and Mrs. James McClary; Mr. and Mrs. Jack Needy; Mr. and Mrs. Jesse Pennock; Mr. and Mrs. Harrison Wilson; Mr. and Mrs. Richard Muldoon, whose log home has served as a prototype for my characters' homestead; Mr. Nigel McKelvey, my research link to Ireland; my father, Mr. B. F. Pennock, who has been my "walking encyclopedia"; and my husband, Ken, who is a never-ending source of encouragement.

CHAPTER ONE

The Burial

―――――――― ∾ ――――――――

Dogwood Creek, December 1868

The boy stood at the window, his nose pressed against the pane, watching the proceedings that would carry his papa away to his bury hole. His left hand formed a fist that rested on the pane near his forehead. With his right hand he pushed at the unruly shock of raven hair that fell over his blue-black eyes. They were reddened from crying, and now and again he brought his nose away from the pane long enough to dab at his eyes with the back of his hand.

Outside, in the grey December morning, he saw his mama being helped onto the wagon seat by their neighbor, Jacob Broom. Behind the second seat, barely visible above the sideboards of the wagon bed, was the coffin that held Lee William Chidester.

The boy, whose rightful name was William John Chidester the II but who had never been called anything but Little John, watched as Cora Broom, Jacob's wife, spread a quilt over Mama's lap. He reasoned that the quilt would protect her from the cold and that she would not come home chilled to the bone as Papa had two weeks ago.

He shuddered and then slowly, deliberately turned his gaze to the horses. Impatiently, they pawed the frozen earth

1

beneath them and snorted out little puffs of steam from their nostrils.

Now he closed his eyes and tried to remember that other horse—the one that had carried his papa home after the great rebellion was over three years ago. The family had all thought Lee William Chidester to be dead—blown to bits in the explosion of the *Sultana* on the Mississippi. But Mama had never believed it. She had said all along that Papa would come home again.

He had come one June morning, riding a great roan horse and looking as pale as a February sun. On that day, Little John could scarcely believe his good fortune to have his papa back from the dead, but he had feared even then that it might not be for long.

He had been six-going-on-seven the day the roan horse came. From the first, the image of his father—back from the grave—haunted him for reasons his young mind could not decipher. There was no doubt in his mind that this was indeed his very own papa—still he did not look as Little John had remembered him. It was as though a great strong man had ridden away to fight in Mr. Lincoln's army and in his place had come this shadow of a man whose eyes carried a look of despair so great that even the boy could read it, albeit he could not put a name to it.

Once Little John had asked Mama, "Was Papa always poor as a snake?" She didn't really answer. She just looked at him carefully and said, "Papa's goin' to be fit as a fiddle, you'll see."

Two summers came and went and the boy followed his papa around as he worked the rocky fields on the Ozark farm that mostly belonged to Grandma MaryAnn. In time Lee William's skin browned under the sun, and his long lanky frame filled out, but the haunted look in his eyes never went away. The boy kept searching them and kept hoping but finally he could bear it no more. He quit looking into his papa's eyes.

In the summer just past, when Little John was nine, he had helped Lee William in the fields as he could, enjoying the feeling that they were becoming partners in toil.

Sometimes in the evening they would sit together with Mama and the girls near the open door of their hilltop cabin to catch the cool air. Papa would tell Mama how the crops looked and what he and Little John had done that day. She would always nod her head and say, "That's good, Lee William. Now, could you play us a tune or two?"

The boy would wait for his father's command to fetch the fiddle, for no one touched it without Lee William's permission. Little John always stood a little straighter when he handed the fiddle to Papa after fetching it from under the bed, for he knew that he was being trusted with his father's most prized possession.

Every night in the summer past, the boy had fallen asleep to the sounds of the ancient fiddle. And every morning he had gulped down his breakfast so that he might be ready to go to the fields with his papa.

The corn crop was especially good this year and Lee William told his young son that it was because he had had such good help.

Deep down, Little John began to hope that his father would always be there and that, one day, they would be real partners on the farm.

Now, standing in the parlor of Grandma MaryAnn's cabin, the boy thought gloomily about how they had come here the week after Thanksgiving because the old woman was ailing and needed watching after.

Then, on the very next day, Papa had gone to gather the last of the corn from the shocks, long dried in their tented rows. He had come in at suppertime, chilled to the bone, for it had been raining for an hour.

The boy shivered, remembering. Papa had stood behind the stove shaking from the cold and Little John had hidden himself in the kitchen, not wanting to look death in the eye.

Papa went to bed with his chill and Mama sent Little John to fetch the doctor. But Papa never got out of his bed again. A week later, he died. It was Little John's tenth birthday.

Now, two days later, they were carrying his papa away.

For three years, the boy had carried the image of his father coming home from the war astride that great roan horse; but this morning, try as he might to hold on to it, he could see only the fresher image of this team and wagon come to carry Papa to his bury hole.

He watched until he could see the wagon no longer. Then, wiping his eyes with the back of his hand, he silently wished that his Uncle Russell Brean Chidester would come. Next to Papa, Uncle Russell was Little John's favorite man in all the world.

Lucy, the boy's mother, had sent for Russell to come, for day and night her ailing husband had called for his brother. Arial, their oldest daughter, had written the letter, for Lucy Chidester could neither read nor write. The boy had taken the letter to Carrick's Mill to meet the mail coach for St. Louis and had waited impatiently for his uncle's arrival ever since.

But it was too late. Uncle Russell had not come and the wagon was hauling Papa away to the graveyard by the schoolhouse up the road.

At ten, Little John was old enough to go to the burying along with his fourteen-year-old sister Amy. But he stayed home with Arial. Partly he stayed to help her take care of twelve-year-old Anna Marie, who was awfully sick, and Grandma MaryAnn, who was dying. Partly he stayed home because he wanted to will his father back. He reasoned that if he never saw them put his papa in the bury hole, he would not have to believe that his papa was dead. One day Papa would come home again astride a great roan horse.

———

From the corner of the room, Grandma MaryAnn Chidester looked up from her bed and stared at the back of the boy's head. For all his young life, she had tried to take away Little John's fears, for she loved him almost more than anything, and besides, she believed that little boys should not be burdened with grown-up worries. Noting how silently he stood watching the wagon carry away his papa—her own seventh son—she sighed heavily and picked at the coverlet on her bed. Then drawing a deep breath for strength, she called to him.

In an instant he was at her bedside.

"Little John," she began, struggling for breath, "it's not easy growing up without a papa, but it can be done. Your grandfather Chidester and your great-grandfather Brean were both very small when their papas died. You must be strong."

"Yes'm," he whispered, but his lips quivered. "Grandma, are you goin' to die, too? And Anna Marie?"

"Anna Marie is not goin' to die, Little John. You'll see."

"But she's so sick. And she can't talk."

MaryAnn tugged at the coverlet and avoided looking at the boy.

"Is it goin' to be a long winter, Grandma?"

"What a question, child!" She stared, wondering at how he had always taken notice of grown-up talk. So many long winters there had been—but for her there was no more worry of the season.

"Is it, Grandma?" the boy persisted.

"Yes, Little John, I'm afraid it is. But you must be brave. When your mama comes home, you must remind her that no matter how long the winter, the spring will always come."

"Why, Grandma?"

"Why what, Little John?"

"Why must I remind Mama?"

"Because it will make her smile. You'll see." Then, reaching slowly, she patted his hand. "Now . . . I have . . . something for you. Please . . . bring . . . the book." She spoke so softly he had to lean closer to hear.

He hurried to the table and fetched the big Bible. Carefully he placed it in her hands and waited.

She had just opened her mouth to speak when Arial called from the bedroom. "Little John, come quick!"

The boy felt a lump rise in his throat and his heart begin to pound as he dashed to the bedroom. *Anna Marie's dyin'*, he thought. *She's dyin' after all. Who cares if spring comes again, anyway?*

Coming into the room he stopped short and stared at the scene before him. Anna Marie was sitting up in bed. "Hello, Little John," she said weakly.

He stood still for a moment, his mouth gaping, and then fell across the bed, hugging his sister to him. He blinked his eyes to keep back the tears. Then, his voice edged with laughter, he said, "Grandma was right after all."

"I reckon Grandma's always right, Little John," Arial said. "But what are you talkin' about?"

"She just now told me Anna Marie would get well." Little John squeezed his ailing sister a little harder.

Arial leaned over and hugged the two of them together. Then, pulling Little John up, she said, "We'd best let her rest a bit now. S'pose you go tell Grandma MaryAnn the good news?"

He nodded. Smiling at Anna Marie, he said, "I'm glad you're gettin' better."

———

Back at his grandmother's bedside, the boy exclaimed, "Grandma, you were right! Anna Marie's talkin' again!" Then, leaning closer, he noticed that her eyes were closed. "Did you hear me, Grandma?" he asked. "Anna Marie is gettin' well."

The old woman's eyes fluttered as she whispered, "You see . . . you see!" In her hand, she clasped a piece of paper. The Bible lay open on her breast. "Little John," she said between labored breaths, "I must . . . tell you something."

He glanced at the paper in her hand and then looked at her.

"Yes'm?"

"You are the seventh child . . . of the . . . seventh son . . . of the seventh child . . . Can you understand that?"

His answer was a question more than a statement. "That I am Papa's seventh child and he was your seventh son?"

"Yes, and . . . "

"And you was a seventh child. I know, Grandma, you're all the time tellin' me that, but what does it mean?"

" . . . means that you're . . . right special . . . when you're old enough . . ." A cough seized her and she motioned him away. As it subsided, she clutched the paper more tightly, lay back on her pillow, and closed her eyes.

From a few feet away the boy watched as the old woman's breathing became fainter. It was so long in between breaths that he wanted to scream at her, "Breathe, Grandma! You're forgettin' to breathe!"

But MaryAnn Chidester was dying, and the boy knew it.

The thought came to him that he alone was left and he wondered frantically if death came to all seventh children in the same season.

Slowly he turned his back to her and crept across the room to the window. He forced great gulps of air into his lungs. Then, reminding himself to keep breathing, he pressed his nose against the window pane once more.

———

Little John was still standing at the window when the Brooms brought Lucy home from the burying. He watched his mama get down, and saw his sister, Amy, ride away with the Brooms as Mama waved good-bye. When she came into the cabin, Little John turned to look at her, but said nothing.

She came to him, her reddened eyes full of sympathy. She pushed back the black bonnet, letting it hang loose about her neck, but made no effort to remove her cloak. At thirty-three, her hair was still the color of corn and she had combed it earlier that day into a bun at the nape of her neck. She smoothed it with her long slender fingers as she explained unnecessarily that Amy had gone home with the Brooms.

Then, laying her hand on the boy's forehead, she asked, "Little John, how come you're breathin' that way?"

"I'm just breathin', Mama!" He jerked his head away.

She studied his face for a moment, but made no effort to check again on the temperature of his forehead. Satisfied that he was not unwell, she asked about Grandma Mary-Ann. He looked at her, fear written in his eyes, but could not speak. She turned from him and crossed to the bed in the corner.

From his position near the window, the boy watched as his mama looked at the form on the bed and then returned to where he stood. Laying a hand on his shoulder, she said, "Little John, your grandma MaryAnn is dead." He could see tears brimming in her eyes once again.

"I knowed she was dyin'."

"How'd you know, Son?"

"She talked queer. Like she was sayin' good-bye—only she never said it." Little John threw his arms around his mama and sobbed into her skirt. Then, standing back, he dug at his eyes with the back of his fists. "Does that mean that I'm goin' to die too, Mama?"

She gasped. "Little John, whatever can you mean? You're as healthy as a horse."

"But I'm the seventh child, like Papa and like Grandma and they died practically together and now I'm the only one left and—"

She crushed him to her. "Son, Son," she whispered over his hysterical sobs. At last when he had grown silent, she kissed him on the cheek and said, "Don't worry none about such a thing again, you hear me? You recollect Papa and Grandma MaryAnn both been real sick. I reckon you're a strong young boy and now you're the man of the house."

9

Remembering the old woman's words, the boy asked, "Does spring always come, Mama?"

He watched the corner of her mouth turn up just a little as she answered. "I reckon Grandma MaryAnn told you to be rememberin' that, did she?"

"Yes'm. She said 'no matter how long the winter, the spring will always come.' She said I was to tell you that and it would make you smile."

"Did it help you to smile?"

"No, ma'am. But Anna Marie did—Mama, I plumb forgot! Anna Marie's talkin' again."

Mama's eyes widened as she asked, "Are you sure?"

"It's true, Mama," Arial said from the bedroom doorway. With finger to lips she motioned them to be quiet. "She's asleep now. I'm going to fix her some broth—she'll likely be hungry when she wakes." Pausing on her way to the kitchen, she added, "If you're ready to take off your cloak and bonnet, I'll hang them for you."

"I clean forgot," Lucy answered. She removed the items and handed them to Arial. "I'll just look in on Anna Marie and then we got to take care of Grandma." Her voice caught and she dabbed at her eyes.

Arial paused at the sight of her mother crying. She looked from Lucy to the still form on the bed in the corner. A look of understanding crept over her face as she mumbled, "I didn't know . . . " Her eyes clouded as she turned away and ran to the kitchen. A moment later she could be heard sobbing softly.

Lucy looked toward the kitchen as if to follow Arial, but turned instead to the bedroom where her youngest daughter slept.

The boy followed her and, almost unconsciously, reached for her hand as they stood there beside Anna Marie's sleeping form. He listened as his mama quietly prayed, "Almighty God, I reckon you knew how much a body could bear. You knew I couldn't bear to have Anna Marie die, too . . . " She bent low to kiss the sleeping girl on the forehead, then, hand in hand, she and Little John left the room.

In the parlor, they stood together beside the body of Grandma MaryAnn.

"Little John," Mama asked, "what was Grandma doin' with the Bible and this paper?"

He shrugged. Fearing that she might ask him to read the paper for her, he walked back to the window. He didn't want to think what might be on the paper. Perhaps it explained about seventh children—perhaps it explained how death came to all seventh children in the same season.

"Little John!" He heard her call, but he took no notice.

"Well, no matter," she said.

Cautiously, he looked around. Her back was to him now. She picked up the paper, smoothed it out, and placed it in her pocket. Then, after removing the Bible, she drew the cover up until it covered Grandma MaryAnn's face.

Arial came into the room and stood beside her mother. "Had we oughta fetch Cora Bennett to help with the layin' out, Mama? Maybe Little John could go—that is, if we could tear him away from the window." She didn't wait for Lucy to answer. Instead she turned to Little John and said impatiently, "I declare you're goin' to wear a hole in the floor before the day's over."

Defying his sister, the boy faced the window and touched his nose to the pane.

"And another thing," Arial continued. "Your nose is fixin' to grow to that pane if you're not careful."

"Don't be raisin' your voice now," Mama said. "Have some respect for the dead and . . ."

Little John didn't hear the rest. His attention was caught by the figure of a man approaching the cabin. He could not see the man's face, for his head was wrapped in a muffler and bent low against the cold. But as the man drew closer, the boy could see that under the heavy winter coat one arm hung straight and limp at the man's side.

He knew of only one man with a useless left arm—his Uncle Russell. "He was run over by a wagon when he was a little boy," Papa had said once long ago. "Never had use of his arm since, but there's not much he can't do with his one good arm."

Forgetting his mama's admonition to speak quietly, Little John yelled, "Uncle Russell's here!"

He rushed to the door to let him in. As soon as the door was closed behind, he locked his arms around his uncle's waist.

"Uncle Russell," he demanded, "whyn't you come sooner?"

"I'm sorry, Son. I truly did come as quick as I could." The man pried himself loose and hunched down a bit to see the boy better as he spoke.

"Hello, Uncle Russell," Arial called and came to stand beside them.

Russell pulled himself up straight and kissed her on the cheek. Then, crossing the room to where his sister-in-law stood, he said, "Hello, Lucy."

His eyes fell on the covered form on the bed. He shook his head and said almost in a whisper, "I'm too late . . . my brother's already dead."

Lucy's eyes filled with tears as she answered. "Dead and buried, Russell . . . This here's your mama—died this mornin' while . . ." She burst into tears and buried her head on his shoulder. "Oh, Russell, what am I goin' to do?"

From his station near the window, the boy watched as Russell wrapped his good arm around Lucy and patted her on the back. Then he turned once more and stuck his nose to the window pane. Only this time he didn't stare into the bleak winter day. This time he scrunched his eyes shut and tried in vain to conjure up the image of the great roan horse that had carried Papa home from the dead.

CHAPTER TWO

Mitchell Callaway

—————————— ❧ ——————————

R ussell Chidester inched lower into the saddle as he
reined his dead brother's horse along Solomon's Ridge.
He bent his neck forward and ducked his head in an
effort to escape the bite of the snow-chilled air. He had drawn
his muffler up, covering his broad, square jaw. Turning just
slightly, he could see his destination on yonder ridge. Over
two miles away, the Bennett home was plainly visible
through the leafless winter trees.

From the first year that the Chidesters had lived on
Dogwood Creek, Russell's mama, MaryAnn, had thought of
Cora Bennett as her closest friend. Cora had laid out the
bodies of Russell's papa and Lee William's infant son over ten
years ago. Two days ago, she had laid out Lee William. Now
Russell would fetch her to perform this last ritual bathing of
his mama.

Tears welled up in his blue-black eyes—eyes that had been
filled with anger when he was a younger man. Now forty, he
was at peace with himself and his eyes had taken on a softer,
almost sympathetic look. Wiping at them now with the
gloved back of his useless hand, he felt relief that he was
alone. At the cabin he had not allowed himself to contemplate

his own grief for he had not wanted Lucy to see him cry. He had, instead, set his mind on comforting her and her children—especially the boy.

He felt deeply troubled remembering Little John's look. There was a sadness there, but more than that, a searching—a searching that was directed at Russell alone. Clearly the boy expected something of him—but what? What could he do? What could anyone do for a ten-year-old whose pa had just been buried?

What he really wants is for his papa to be alive again, Russell thought, remembering the summer after the rebellion was over. He had been with the family, helping with the crops, when his brother had come home, all gaunt looking and almost too skinny to throw a shadow. Russell almost smiled, thinking of that day—Little John had fetched him from the field, shouting that his papa had come home.

There had been a great celebration around the table that night and, soon afterward, Russell had returned to St. Louis to his job with Mr. Eads. But he had seized every opportunity to come to Dogwood Creek to visit the family—especially his brother and the boy.

Russell had never shared the family's love for Dogwood Creek. He had been more than satisfied working in St. Louis, but separation from his younger brother had created a void in his life that had never been filled. And now Lee William was gone—dead and buried.

He sighed deeply, asking himself what his sister-in-law had asked not an hour ago. *What am I going to do? How can I bear to lose both Mama and Lee William at once?* His shoulders slumped and once more he wiped the back of his glove across his eyes.

———

Ten minutes later, he rode into the Bennetts' yard. Pulling himself up straight, he made an effort to regain his composure.

After tying the horse at the gate, he walked across the porch to the front door of the Bennetts' frame house.

Logan answered his knock. "Russell Chidester!" he exclaimed, thrusting out his hand and urging Russell to come in out of the cold. As they shook hands, Russell observed silently that Logan's grip belied the fact that he was getting on in years. Greying hair framed his wrinkled face, but he stood straight as any man and, from what Russell had heard, still worked his farm by himself.

"I'm sorry 'bout your brother, Russell," the older man said. "Lee William was mighty well liked in these parts. Didn't see you at the buryin'—you just get here?"

Russell nodded. Then seeing Cora enter the room, he greeted her, "Hello, Cora." Unlike her husband, Cora Bennett carried herself with a slight stoop now. In spite of this, and the weight she had added over the years, she still walked briskly.

She greeted him warmly, offering her sympathy for the loss of his brother. Then, with characteristic understanding, she asked, "Is somethin' wrong, Russell? Not likely you'd be payin' a neighborly visit, with your brother not three hours in his grave, unless somethin' was wrong. Is it Anna Marie . . . or MaryAnn?" She frowned.

Russell held his hat in his good hand. He worked it between his fingers as he stared at the floor and tried to speak. Finally he swallowed hard and, looking at Cora, said, "It's Mama—died this morning while they were burying Lee William."

"I'll get my cloak, Russell. I'll come this minute." Cora laid a hand on his shoulder. "I'm sorry. It's never been a secret 'round these parts how much you thought of your brother. And that boy, Little John—ever'body knows how he looks up to you. Your mama—she was a good woman and she was mighty proud of you. When she talked about you she always made me wish I had a son just like you."

"Thank you for that, Cora." Russell's voice was quiet as he replied. "It wasn't always that way. What I mean is, there were times when Mama and I didn't see eye to eye but . . . " He turned his glance away.

Cora patted him on the shoulder and, mumbling that Logan would bring her along directly, hurried out of the room.

The two men stood silently for a moment. At length, Logan cleared his throat and suggested that he could round up some men to dig the grave. "We can have it ready by afternoon tomorrow," he offered.

Having settled the matter, Russell took his leave and mounted Tony, Lee William's horse, once more.

At the end of his ride, he came again to Solomon's Ridge, passing the empty hilltop cabin that Lee William had built for Lucy. He was accustomed to seeing it empty in the winter now and then, for his brother's family had often stayed with his mama in times of illness or severe weather. Now he wondered what would happen. Would Lucy move back to the hilltop place? If so, what would happen to Mama's cabin—the home that his pa and he and Lee William had built the second spring after they moved from Indiana?

He speculated over the question while he unsaddled the horse and put him in the barn. Still pondering, he walked down the hill to the cabin. Suddenly a movement caught his attention. Pausing to look, he let out a low whistle. Tethered to the gate was as fine a saddle horse as he had ever seen. *Now where would anybody around these parts get a horse like that?* he wondered.

Once inside the cabin, Russell's unspoken questions were both answered.

Arial was sitting at the table quietly talking to a young man. The brightness of her eyes told Russell that the stranger was not merely paying a neighborly visit. He stood up when Russell entered the room.

"Uncle Russell," Arial said, "this is Mitchell Callaway."

Tall and slender, Arial favored her dead papa, having inherited both his curly dark brown hair and brown eyes. As she introduced the young man, even her voice seemed to smile.

"Pleased to make your acquaintance, Mr. Chidester," Mitchell greeted him. "Arial's told me a lot about you."

Russell studied his face and wondered why Arial had never told him anything about Mitchell Callaway. He offered his hand, but said nothing.

"Mitch and I are getting married the day after Christmas," Arial explained. "That is, we was planning to. We're goin' to live in Mama and Papa's cabin. Mama's goin' to live with—" Arial paused, her voice catching, and then continued, "—that is, they was planning on livin' with Grandma MaryAnn. Only now it will just be Mama and the girls and Little John."

Russell looked at his niece and then at Mitchell. He wasn't at all sure he liked what he saw—*too dandy for Dogwood Creek somehow,* he observed. He judged the young man to be perhaps twenty years of age. A pronounced jawline was broken at the chin by a deep dimple. He wore his thick black hair parted on the side but there was too much of it to comb down properly. It was cut close to his head on the sides, showing his well-proportioned ears. Beneath his neatly trimmed mustache the corners of his mouth turned up so that he looked like he was permanently happy with the world.

It's easy to see how a young girl would . . . Russell mused.

"Uncle Russell?" Arial's voice interrupted his thoughts. "Uncle Russell, did you hear me?"

"I was thinking of something, Arial. What did you say?"

"Mitch and I, we don't know what's proper. Do you think it's all right for us to be gettin' married? I mean we don't want to show no disrespect for Papa and Grandma."

"Did your papa and grandma approve, Arial?"

A look passed between Arial and Mitchell Callaway.

Russell waited for his niece to answer. When she did, she looked him directly in the eye and, with a hint of determination, said, "I reckon they approved of Mitch as much as they'd approve of anyone I decided to marry."

"What she means, sir, is that it was hard for them to let her get married."

Russell ignored Callaway's remark and once more directed his question to Arial. "What does your mama say?"

"Mama helped us make the plans and all. Grandma Mary-Ann even suggested that the family move in with her so Mitch and I could have the hilltop cabin. But that was before—I mean I haven't said anything to Mama since . . . I just can't bring myself to bother her about it. It's been so hard on her with ever'body so sick."

"If you want, I'll talk to your mama."

Arial's gratitude was plain as she smiled at her uncle. "We'd be obliged if you would."

For a moment Russell looked at Callaway and wondered whether he should satisfy his curiosity about the horse—such a young man for a fine horse like that! But he thought better of it and went instead to hang his wraps on the pegs behind the cookstove. Then he left the room in search of Lucy. He found her sitting beside Anna Marie, feeding her broth.

He bent to kiss the girl on the forehead and she hugged him weakly. "I'm glad to see you're able to sit up and take nourishment," he said enthusiastically. But privately, he searched the pale thin face for signs that she would recover. He studied the dark circles around her eyes and the lips that were cracked from the fever that had now run its course. She was babbling something to him that he had not heard. Rather than admit to his inattention, he smiled at her and then, with mock severity, ordered, "Eat your broth."

Turning to Lucy, he explained that Cora would be along directly.

When Anna Marie had finished her broth, Lucy rose to leave, motioning Russell to follow. They walked into the parlor to a spot near the window.

"She'll be all right, won't she, Russell? Doctor comes again in two days. She looks so much better." Lucy's eyes pleaded for reassurance.

"I'll admit I was a mite worried," he replied. "But I'm sure the worst is over. When the doctor comes he'll likely be pleased with what he sees."

She smiled at him. "I'm obliged to you, Russell, for coming. Seems like every time we got troubles, you're such a help."

Embarrassed, he glanced away momentarily. Shuffling his feet, he reported on the arrangements he and Logan had made about the digging. "He'll get word to Old Man Carrick at the mill to make the coffin. And I expect Logan will stay the night and sit up with the body. We'll spell each other . . ." His voice caught. He turned to face her and for the second time in three hours caught her closely to him. Only this time he blurted out the question: "Lucy, Lucy, what will we ever do without them?"

At the sound of footsteps on the porch, they drew themselves apart. A cold draft swept into the room as Russell opened the door for the Bennetts. After an exchange of greetings, Cora took charge. She asked for a pan of warm water, soap, and a supply of clean rags. She pulled the curtain across the door of the bedroom where Anna Marie rested and shooed everyone else into the kitchen.

Russell noted that Arial was still seated at the table with Mitchell Callaway. He followed Logan's glance as the older man turned to Callaway.

"Afternoon, Mitchell," Logan greeted him. "I saw your horse outside. Reckoned you might be here."

Mitchell rose politely. "Afternoon, Mr. Bennett."

"If you're ridin' back to the mill soon, you might take a message to Carrick for us." His tone implied that this was more than a suggestion.

"If I can be of help—" Mitchell began.

Logan interrupted. "Tell him we're needin' another coffin by afternoon tomorrow. Tell him it's for MaryAnn Chidester."

"I'll do that," Mitchell said. With a glance at Arial and a nod to Russell he left. Logan followed soon afterwards.

Russell sat with Arial, silently watching as Lucy busied herself at the stove.

"You must be starved, Russell!" she said. "You had such a long ride and all. Fact is, it's high time we all ate. Little John went to fetch Amy from the Brooms and to tell 'em that your mama died." Her voice sounded higher than normal and her words tumbled out much too quickly. She jerked pans of leftover biscuits and cornbread from the warming oven. She stirred the rabbit stew that was simmering on the back of the stove, splashing the hot juice on her hand as she did so. Dashing to the wash basin by the door, she grabbed the dipper from the water bucket, and poured some cool spring water over her hand. Then, moving back to the stove, she checked the stew once more and said, "This'll be ready 'fore long . . . " Suddenly she clapped her hand to her mouth as a muffled sob escaped.

Arial rose at once to go to her mother's side, but Russell sat still at the table. *It's the body,* he thought, staring out the window. *Knowing that Cora's in there washing Mama's body is making Lucy crazy.* He wished he could think of something to say. He wished he didn't feel so awkward. He was relieved to see Little John and Amy coming up the lane. He met them at the kitchen door so they would not intrude on Cora's business in the parlor.

Their greetings were interrupted as Cora came into the kitchen. "It's done," she announced, glancing at the five of them one by one.

"We're obliged to you, Cora." Lucy paused to wipe her eyes before continuing, "supper's on the table. You'll eat with us?"

But Cora declined, saying that she would hurry on home to fix Logan's supper. "He'll be back directly to sit up," she said as she left.

They ate with hardly a sound, and when they had finished, it seemed there was as much left as when they had begun.

———————

Logan had not yet returned when Little John and the girls went to bed. Russell and Lucy sat alone in the dimly lit kitchen. He stared into the darkness, saying nothing. He was hardly aware of her presence until she commented softly, "Life can be hard, can't it, Russell?"

He nodded, wondering if he dared add to her burden of grief by telling her his troubled thoughts. He cleared his throat. Looking her directly in the eyes, he said, "Tell me about Mitchell—where'd he come from?"

"Reckon nobody knows that, Russell. He just come to the mill one day. Old Man Carrick set his few slaves free you know, even 'fore the rebellion was over. Gave 'em deed to some land up the holler and they're farmin' fer themselves. So Carrick, he needed someone to work at the mill store and he hired Mitchell first day he come to Dogwood Creek. Arial met him there next time she wuz at the store."

"It's none of my business," Russell acknowledged, "but . . ."

"But what, Russell?"

"He doesn't strike me as good husband material for Arial. What did my brother think of this marriage? Did he approve?"

"Well, you might know how Lee William would be—he was all the time thinkin' that nobody was good enough fer his girls."

"Was he ever suspicious of Mitchell?"

"Suspicious? Why should he be?"

"People don't just pass through here, Lucy. Didn't you ever wonder how Callaway came to be here?"

Lucy shrugged.

Russell pressed further. "And what about that horse?"

"What about it?"

"That's a mighty fancy horse for such a young fella. Most men work half a lifetime to get a mount like that. And you must have noticed his sidearm . . . "

"I reckon I have. He's never without it," Lucy replied.

When she made no further response, Russell commented, "Arial's not so sure they should get married right away."

"She's upset about her papa and Grandma MaryAnn."

"Probably so," Russell said, then cautiously suggested, "perhaps they should postpone it for a while."

"Out of respect for your mama and Lee William?"

He stared away into the dark corner of the room for a minute before replying. "I just think it's a good idea for her to wait." Seeing that Lucy was not going to respond, he asked, "What do you think, Lucy? You're her mama."

"I can't hardly think about it, Russell. I admit I'm not real easy 'bout Mitchell Callaway, but it's been right hard to think 'bout anythin', 'cept takin' care of the sick ones. It wouldn't hurt for 'em to wait awhile longer. But I don't aim to tell her what to do." She studied Russell's face and then continued, "Maybe you oughta tell her how you feel. Maybe you oughta talk to her."

Russell looked at her then and saw a face creased with weariness. He saw vacant eyes staring at him with the gaze of one who could hardly concentrate on the present for the pain of the recent past and the dread of the uncertain future.

Having seen her thus, he made up his mind.

Tomorrow, he would ask Arial to put off her marriage to Mitchell Callaway.

CHAPTER THREE

Grandma MaryAnn's Paper

───────── ❧ ─────────

Little John had not wanted to come to the burying—had declared that he would stay home with Anna Marie. But Lucy had decided that Amy should stay and that both Arial and the boy should come.

He stood there now, his eyes fixed on the gaping hole the men had dug for Grandma MaryAnn. He dared not turn his head for fear he would see the fresh-turned grave where his papa lay.

Carefully, without the slightest deflection of his eyes, he stepped backward against his uncle Russell. At once he felt a strong hand gripping his shoulder. He quieted at the touch, and they stood thus together—so close that they cast a single shadow under the pale winter sun.

Beyond MaryAnn Chidester's still empty hole, the boy could see the ancient graves—the first ones to be dug in this burying ground next to the schoolhouse. He knew that the oldest grave belonged to Grandma MaryAnn's husband—the first William John Chidester for whom he was named. Cautiously, he looked at the tiny grave next to Grandpa Chidester's—the grave where the baby boy lay. He had been told that this baby would have been his big brother had he lived.

It was hard for Little John to put a form to either the grandfather or the baby because they were already in their graves before he was born. It was far easier to imagine that he—the last of the seventh children would be next.

Old Man Carrick stood to read from the Bible and the sight of the Book brought a vision to the boy of his dying grandma lying on the bed with the Book open on her breast and the paper clutched in her hand. He shuddered, and at once the hand on his shoulder tightened.

He closed his eyes as Carrick prayed and when he opened them, he saw that the men were lowering the box into the hole.

His eyes widened in terror. As the first clods of frozen earth thudded on the wooden coffin, he clapped his hands over his ears. Then, bursting into tears, he turned and threw his arms around his uncle.

He stood there with his face pressed against Russell for a long while, taking no notice of the muted sounds of people milling about, talking quietly and loading themselves onto their wagons. He was conscious only of the feel of a strong right hand gently rubbing his shoulder. He scrunched his eyes together and imagined that Uncle Russell was never going back to his job in St. Louis—that he would stay on Dogwood Creek forever.

At last, Russell spoke. "They're all fixin' to leave, Son." The boy stood back and wiped his eyes on his coat sleeve. Then, putting his gloved hand in his uncle's, he walked toward the Brooms' wagon. His mama and Arial were already seated on the second seat behind the Brooms. He and Russell sat together on the end of the wagon with their backs to the others.

As they watched the schoolhouse slowly disappear, Russell threw his good arm over the boy's shoulders and asked, "Are you in school, Little John?"

"Ain't no school."

"Why is that? There's a perfectly good schoolhouse here."

The boy didn't know for certain, but he did know it had something to do with a loyalty oath and he was quick to tell his uncle that it didn't matter, for he could already read and write.

Russell promptly told him that it did matter, that he must keep up with his books even if he had no school to attend and then lectured him about Mr. Eads who was building a great bridge across the Mississippi and who had learned everything he knew from studying on his own.

Little John listened politely and hesitantly suggested that if his uncle would come to Dogwood Creek to teach that he would study hard.

Russell looked at the boy intently, but said not a word. After a moment he turned to Lucy and questioned her about the loyalty oath business—why should it affect the school on Dogwood Creek where folks never paid any attention to what went on in the outside world? Besides, he argued, the oath had been repealed.

She explained to him then that the teacher who had come from the next county over did pay attention to such things and that he couldn't swear he had never had any dealings with the Confederates so he had to leave. As for the repeal, they all knew about it but it would have been better had it come sooner—before the only teacher they could find was forced to leave and find work of another sort.

Somewhat exasperated, Russell turned to the boy and reminded him, "You have all of your grandpa William John's schoolbooks. See that you study this winter."

"You mean by myself, without no teacher?"

"Yes, by yourself," Russell said firmly, "and don't forget what I told you about Mr. Eads."

The noise of the wagon wheels clattering along the uneven ruts of Grandma MaryAnn's lane prevented further conversation. Little John snuggled closer to his uncle and examined the road over which they had come. When the wagon came to a halt, he jumped down. Facing forward for the first time, he spied a horse and rider at the gate.

His tear-swollen eyes brightened as he explained to his uncle, "That's Mitch—Arial's feller."

"I know," Russell responded. "We've met."

Mitchell Callaway dismounted and tied the reins to a fence post. Then, tipping his broadbrim hat to Lucy, he said, "Afternoon, ma'am."

"Afternoon, Mitchell," she replied.

The boy stared, transfixed as Callaway reached for the women, first Lucy, then Arial, and helped them down. As he stood watching, Little John moved his facial muscles, checking with his finger to see if the corners of his mouth turned up. He poked a gloved finger into the center of his chin and, without turning his head, said to Russell, "Ain't he somethin'? When I get big, I wanta be just like him." Still intent on Callaway, he did not see the frown that crossed his uncle's face.

Without waiting for a response, Little John hurried to Mitch's side, asking at once if he were coming in.

"Of course he's comin' in," Arial answered over the clatter of the Brooms' departing wagon.

30

"Come on then," the boy urged, tugging at Mitch's arm.

But Lucy caught Little John by the shoulder at that moment and explained that Uncle Russell wanted to talk to Arial and Mitch. Giving him no time to protest, she pulled him into the house, leaving the others standing by the gate.

In a few minutes, they came in. Arial and Mitch went directly to the parlor where Arial curtly dismissed Little John from the room, saying she and Mitch had things to talk about. Reluctantly, the boy followed his uncle into the kitchen where Lucy and Amy busied themselves with supper preparations. Supper was already on the table when Arial came to the kitchen saying that Mitch had gone home.

"He never even said good-bye!" the boy protested.

"Sorry, Little John. It's just that we had to decide about some things and . . . "

"Decide about what?"

"Little John, mind your manners with your sister," Lucy scolded. "Don't be poking into what's no business of yours."

"It's all right, Mama. I was aimin' to tell you all at supper anyhow. Mitch and I decided not to get married this month."

Little John stared, wide-eyed, at his sister. "You're not goin' to marry Mitch?" he asked anxiously.

"I didn't say that," Arial answered. "We're goin' to wait awhile, that's all."

Relieved, the boy pressed his sister for details. "When do you aim to get married?"

Arial shrugged. "Don't know." She looked directly at Russell. "We'll wait awhile, but we won't wait a whole year."

Before Little John could question her further, Amy came alongside him and whispered in his ear. Leaving the kitchen at once, he disappeared through the parlor into the bedroom. There he found Anna Marie dressed and waiting to join the

31

others. He walked with her back to the kitchen, coming to the doorway just as the others were sitting down.

Amy, her eyes gleaming, announced loudly, "Ever'body! This here is Miss Anna Marie Chidester, come to supper for the first time in two weeks!"

Beaming, Anna Marie sat down as her surprised audience burst into applause.

Lucy shushed them. "I reckon we're forgettin' that Grandma MaryAnn's not three hours in her grave. Likely we're not bein' very respectful." But she greeted her youngest daughter with smiling eyes as she continued, "Still, we're glad to see you up . . . "

"I reckon Grandma wouldn't care, Mama," Little John interrupted. "She told me that Anna Marie would get well . . . likely she'd want us to be happy about it."

"The boy's right, Lucy," Russell said.

Lucy dabbed the corner of her apron to her eyes as she asked Russell to say a prayer before they ate.

───────────

That night, the boy slept in a cot beside the bed where Grandma MaryAnn had died. Amy had aired out the bedding and remade the bed, suggesting that Little John sleep in it and give his loft room to Uncle Russell. But the boy had protested, a look of terror in his eyes at the mention of Grandma's bed. Russell had spoken up at once, saying that he would sleep in the bed and, if Little John wanted, he could pull the extra cot alongside and sleep next to him.

He lay there now, staring sleepily through the kitchen doorway to the table where his uncle and his mother sat. They talked quietly in the dim lamplight, but he could make out most of the words.

He saw his mama take a paper from her pocket and hand it to Russell. Knowing that it must be the note from Grandma MaryAnn and that his mama would be asking Uncle Russell to read it aloud, he clapped his hands over his ears and closed his eyes. He didn't want to hear anything about seventh children.

When next he opened his eyes, he could see that his uncle was not reading. Slowly he took his hands off his ears. He heard them then, but with little understanding of what they said. "Find a place to put it, Lucy. Keep it until it's time," Russell said softly.

"I know just the place. I'll see that it's done."

The boy yawned and closed his eyes. He fell asleep wishing with all his heart that Uncle Russell would stay on Dogwood Creek.

———

He had been asleep for an hour when Lucy and Russell came into the parlor, and stood before the fireplace where the painting of the Irish grandmother hung. He did not see his uncle take the painting down, hold it while his mother stuffed the paper under the back of the frame, and rehang it once more. Nor was he conscious of Lucy bending low to kiss him on the forehead before she and Russell returned to the kitchen to talk.

Russell listened attentively as Lucy spoke. "Seein' that paintin' of your great-grandmother—

"Mama's great-grandmother. My great-great-grandmother," Russell corrected her.

Lucy nodded and began again. "Seein' the picture of your great-great-grandmother reminds me. There's somethin' that needs to be done. Could you write to your mama's brother, George Brean, and tell him about her . . . and about Lee William? I could ask one of the girls to do it, but . . . "

"No need of that, Lucy," he interrupted. "I'll take care of it."

A smile played about the corners of her mouth as she asked, "Russell, do you recollect the other picture paintin'?"

"How could I forget it?" he asked, half smiling himself. "We had been told all our lives that there was another painting, left behind in Ireland. My grandfather was all the time telling us that we had family still in Ireland and that when they came to America they would bring the other painting with them. I only half believed it. But when Lee William came home from the war bringing Cousin Casey with him . . . " He paused and they both laughed lightly at the memory.

"I won't ever forget the look on your mama's face the night Cousin Casey unwrapped that picture."

"Or how we all trooped into the other room and made a regular ceremony out of hanging it!" Russell added.

"It hung there for three months, until George and Cousin Casey went to Indiana."

Suddenly Russell sat up straight. "Lucy!" he exclaimed. "We might find some help for you on the farm this year. Last I heard, Cousin Casey was still with George. If George can get other help, maybe Casey would be willing to come to Dogwood Creek to help with the crops this year. I'll ask when I write."

Lucy's eyes clouded. "It's a worry all right, wonderin' what to do. Little John's not big enough to farm this place."

Russell looked at her soberly. "I can send money and, likely as not, Casey will see his way clear to come for the season.

But I'm not sure that will be enough." Russell stared away from the light.

"Russell," Lucy said softly.

But he made no response.

"Russell, I'm obliged to you. But you got no call to worry. It's not your problem."

"It *is* my problem. Lee William was my brother. And I aim to see that his family is properly cared for." He blinked furiously and refused to look at her as he spoke.

"Russell, look at me." Lucy reached out to touch his hand. But he pulled it away and covered his eyes.

"It's hard for me, Lucy. I'm a grown man. It's hard to have you see me cry."

"I've seen men cry before."

"I reckon you have at that." Russell wiped his eyes, then abruptly asked, "Lucy, are you sure you want to stay in this godforsaken place? Just because my brother and my mama wouldn't leave is no cause for you to stay. It's bound to be hard for you."

"I see you ain't changed in that respect."

"In what respect?"

"You're all the time callin' this a 'godforsaken place.' "

"Well what do you call it? You can't get a teacher to come. There's no church for miles around."

"We got our farm and we got the family Bible. Little John and the girls read it to me. So I reckon God hasn't forsaken us yet."

"It's just a figure of speech, Lucy."

"You'd best find a new one."

He looked up, a bit startled at her tone. He wasn't accustomed to hearing her speak that directly. He was still contemplating the meaning of her abruptness when Lucy took up the conversation once more.

"As for it bein' hard, you're right. But we'll manage somehow. We got to. I got to think about what Lee William and his mama wanted—for the boy and all, don't you see?"

He followed her gaze towards the parlor where they had so recently put the paper for safekeeping. She sighed deeply and concluded, "What else can I do, Russell?"

He looked at her thoughtfully. "I don't know, Lucy," he replied. "I just don't know."

CHAPTER FOUR

An Unexpected Rider

Lucy emptied the water bucket into the iron teakettle on the back of the stove. Wrapping her cloak around her, she grabbed the empty pail and headed for the front door. Before she could lay her hand on the knob, the door opened, and Little John came into the room.

"Chickens are fed, Mama," he announced. He reached for the bucket. "I'll go to the springhouse for you," he said. Before Lucy could protest, the boy was out the door again, hurrying away on his errand.

She watched him briefly through the window. Then, shaking her head, she withdrew her cloak and rehung it.

I'm sorry I ever told him that he was the man of the house now that his papa's gone, she thought. *It's been over two months and he ain't stopped movin' yet—hardly takes time to eat anymore.*

Every morning since the week after they buried Lee William, Lucy had watched the boy gulp down his breakfast and, without once being reminded, hurry out to do the chores. He fetched the wood and water, helped with the milking, fed the cows and led them to water, and fed and watered the chickens. Only when it was time to study Grandpa Chidester's schoolbooks did she have to prod him. Every night she fetched the books from the shelf, handed them to the boy, and reminded him, "I promised Uncle Russell I'd see that you did your books."

He would sit then with Anna Marie and together they worked on their lessons. He had always been close to Anna Marie—had worried over her so when she was sick. Lucy smiled gratefully at the thought of the two of them. *Leastways he has someone to talk to,* she mused. *He for sartin don't say much to the rest of us anymore.*

She was satisfied that he was learning. He had advanced to the next reader. "I reckon I hadn't oughta complain," she muttered as she began gathering together the ingredients for gingerbread. "But it's a worrisome thing to watch him staring off into nowhere, come night time."

"Mama?" Anna Marie stood at the parlor doorway, dustrag in hand. "Who you talkin' to, Mama?"

Embarrassed, Lucy said, "Nobody child. Just thinkin' out loud."

" 'Bout Little John?"

"Now how would you be knowin' that?" Lucy asked.

"I heard you say somethin' 'bout him starin' off into nowhere."

"I see," Lucy said thoughtfully. Then, feeling a need to explain to the girl, she added, "It's not as if he does it once in a while. I reckon it happens as reg'lar as the sun goes down over Solomon's Ridge. If I didn't know better, I'd think he was in a trance."

"Yes'm." Anna Marie's eyes widened as she answered. She shuffled her feet and wadded the dustrag around in her hands. She chewed on the corner of her lip as she met her mother's gaze.

"Somethin' you want to say, child?" Lucy prodded her.

"Yes'm." She bit her lip again.

"Then now's as good a time as any." Lucy tried to speak gently, but she was beginning to feel impatient.

"It's just that I know why he does that . . . "

"Little John, you mean?"

The girl nodded.

"You know why he's all the time starin' off at night?"

"Yes'm." She hesitated once more, then blurted out, "He's talkin' to Papa."

Lucy gasped. Setting her flour sifter down, she walked to Anna Marie, took her by the shoulder, and led her into the bedroom.

"Sit down here, child," she said, motioning to the bed. Obediently, the girl sat. Lucy sat beside her, took her hand in her own and said, "Now tell me what you're talkin' 'bout. And tell me quietly 'cause Little John's likely to be back any time from the spring."

"Yes'm." Anna Marie drew a deep breath before she began. "Little John, he told me one time that he imagines Papa comin' home again like he did after the rebellion was over. He imagines him ridin' that big roan horse. And he . . . you know . . . kinda talks to Papa in his mind sometimes."

"I see."

Lucy looked away from the girl then. She stared at the floor and recalled a long-forgotten image from her childhood. She was playing her favorite game once again—having supper with Mama. She saw herself laying out the imaginary meal and "talking" to the mother who was never really there—the mother who had died when Lucy was born. She shook her head sadly and muttered, "Poor young'un." A wave of fear washed over her as she wondered if the boy could go

39

mad pretending that his papa wasn't dead, that he was coming home again on the roan horse that belonged to Cousin Casey.

"Mama?" Anna Marie's voice broke into Lucy's thoughts. The girl tugged at her mother's hand as she spoke. "Mama?"

"Yes, child?"

"You won't tell Little John I told you, will you?"

Lucy studied a minute before she answered. "It ain't healthy for Little John to be pretendin' his papa is alive when he knows he's dead and buried. Do you understand that, child?"

"Yes'm, but . . . " The girl's eyes were pleading now.

Lucy shrugged. "But there's no need to tell him what you said. It can be our secret."

Anna Marie's eyes brightened and Lucy hugged her. "Now, we'd best get back to work," she said and hurried back to the kitchen.

The waterbucket was in its place, but Little John was nowhere around. *Gone to the barn*, Lucy thought. *Gone on to his next round of chores*. She picked up her sifter once more and returned to her gingerbread making.

Two hours later Little John came in. "I been out checking the field, Mama," he said. "We need to plow soon."

"You're not goin' to do that job by yourself, Little John." She was at once sorry that she had said it. How could she tell him there would be someone to help him until she knew for sure—until the letter came from Indiana? The boy had enough problems without her making promises she couldn't keep.

She needn't have worried. Distracted by the aroma coming from the table, he ignored her remark.

"Can I have some now, Mama?" he asked as he sniffed the fresh-baked gingerbread she had set there.

Glad that he would eat something, she cut him a generous piece and set it on a plate.

When he had finished the last crumb, she smiled at him and asked, "Why don't you take your papa's horse and ride down to the mill? I'm needin' a sack of beans and you can check for mail. Arial will help you saddle him."

———

She sent him three times that week to check for mail, but the expected letter did not come. She worried that it might not come at all and there would be no one to do the plowing.

Returning from his third trip, he reported to her that he had seen Logan Bennett. Lucy was sitting with the two younger girls, patching, and she did not look up until the boy said that Bennett had suggested he might help with the Chidester plowing next week if he got through with his own in time.

"There! You see," she exclaimed, a look of relief on her face, "you don't have to do it by yourself."

Her look turned to one of dismay when he answered, "I reckon next week's too late. I aim to start tomorrow."

"Be patient, a day or two . . . " Then she asked hopefully, "Was there a letter today, Little John?"

"No, Mama, there wasn't."

She sighed. "I've been expectin' a letter from your grandma MaryAnn's brother, George."

"I remember Uncle George," Little John volunteered. "He come during the rebellion to help Grandma on the farm,

41

didn't he? He was here when Papa come home on that big roan horse . . . "

"Yes he was."

"And Uncle Russell was here. And Papa brought along Cousin Casey from Ireland . . . " The boy looked wistful, remembering.

Lucy nodded. "One month it was just me and Grandma MaryAnn tryin' to run this farm and next month we had four men workin' the place. 'Course your pa didn't do much work that summer. And you . . . well you was a little tyke, but you took care of that horse every day until Casey and George left for Indiana."

"The horse that brought Papa home." It was a statement, not a question, and the boy had a faraway look in his eyes as he spoke.

A frown crossed Lucy's face. Instinctively, she glanced toward Anna Marie. But the girl appeared not to notice her brother's expression.

As Lucy watched, the girl blurted out, " 'Pears to me, Little John would have more help this summer if Arial and Mitch was married. Mitch could help with the crops."

Amy looked up then. "If you ask me," she said, "Mitch is near enough family even if him and Arial's not married yet. I think he could help if he had a mind . . . "

She was cut off by a low gasp from the doorway. Arial stood there, her face flushed and her eyes misty. "Mitch is never goin' to be a farmer," she said defensively. "Besides he has his own job to worry about at Carrick's Mill."

Anna Marie snipped, "And I reckon that's worry enough for one man—what with all his trips away. Seems he's gone more than he's at the mill."

"He has to go away, Anna Marie. He's got other jobs he has to take care of."

Lucy had sat quietly, taking in the conversation. Now she spoke, directing her remarks to her oldest daughter. "It does seem to me, Arial, that Mitch is goin' away all the time. I don't recollect you sayin' what he does."

Arial's face colored even deeper, as she answered. "Don't know, Mama. Mitch—he don't talk about it."

Lucy held her peace then. She eyed Anna Marie evenly and, looking from her to Amy, said, "That's enough talk 'bout Mitch. S'pose we let Arial handle her own business."

———

The next morning Little John finished his breakfast hurriedly. Through a mouthful of mush, he declared, "If we aim to have any oats this year, I need to start plowin' today."

Lucy opened her mouth to protest, then thought better of it. "We can't put it off any longer. But you can't do it by yourself, Son. I'll go along . . . "

"No you won't. Papa always said it ain't fittin' for a woman to plow." Then, looking at Arial, he said, "I'd be obliged though, if you could help me harness the mules."

He swallowed his last bite, grabbed his cap and jumper, and ran out the back door with Arial following behind him.

When Arial returned a short while later she had tears in her eyes. "I wanted to go with him, Mama. But he wouldn't have it."

Reading her daughter's face, Lucy knew there was something more that was bothering her. She waited.

"I helped him harness the mules and showed him how to set the plow on edge to get it to the field. I told him to leave the plow in the field tonight and not to try to bring it in. I told him I would bring him dinner . . . " Arial burst into tears. Throwing her arms around her mama, she sobbed, "I'm sorry, Mama, I truly am!"

"Arial, whatever do you mean? You got no call to be sorry. You did what you could. He's bound to do it. He'll have to learn by himself."

"It's not that, Mama," Arial said, dabbing at her eyes. "I know how ever'body feels about Mitch—how he ought to be helpin' Little John and all. But Mitch . . . well he just can't."

Lucy looked at the girl carefully. "Arial, I s'pose your mind's made up, so I'll not be tellin' you what to do . . . only it's not fittin' to marry a man you have to apologize for, and if you're bound to marry him, don't start explainin' for Mitch 'fore you're even married. And don't go takin' on extra work to make up for what you think people expect of him." Then, a bit more kindly, she added, "Anyway, it ain't Mitch's problem."

They talked no more of the matter, but at the end of the day when they heard Little John bringing the mules in from the field, Arial raced up to the barn to meet him. Soon the boy came in without her, explaining that she was taking care of the animals for him.

Lucy tried not to notice the look of discouragement on his face as he sank into the nearest chair. When she asked how the plowing went, he hung his head and said that likely no one on Dogwood Creek had ever seen such crooked furrows.

———

On the sixth day of plowing, he came in early. He walked slowly through the back door, stopping to drink from the dipper. Then without saying a word he walked to the parlor and slumped into the rocker near the window.

Lucy followed him, a great fear rising at the sight of him. "You're tired," she began. "You're workin' too hard."

He smiled halfheartedly, but said nothing.

"How'd the plowing go?" she asked him then.

Tears filled his eyes. "The furrows ain't gettin' any straighter, Mama. And I haven't got half as much plowed as I should." He rubbed his sleeve across his dampened cheeks. "I spent most of the afternoon rubbing the dirt and rust off the plow with my heel to make it scour better. I quit early 'cause it still ain't scouring right. I brought the plow to the barn and put some axle grease on its mole board."

Arial stood nearby listening and emphatically assumed the blame for the dull plow, saying that she should never have told him to leave it in the field. Lucy noticed how the boy only half listened. He leaned his head back and closed his eyes.

She lay a hand on his shoulder. "Little John, we got a surprise for you." She turned to Arial. "Do you still have the letter in your pocket?"

Arial nodded, then handed the letter to her brother. "Here," she said. "Read for yourself. It's mighty good news." The boy opened his eyes and took the letter from her.

"I'll read it directly," he said and closed his eyes again.

"But Little John . . . " Arial started to protest.

"Never mind," Lucy told her. "Leave him be."

In the kitchen, they set about getting supper ready.

Ten minutes later, they heard a horse whinny from the direction of the lane and hurried together to the kitchen window to catch a glimpse of the approaching rider. It was a man astride a great roan horse.

"At last!" Lucy exclaimed, hugging Arial as she spoke.

Suddenly from the parlor, they heard Little John. "It's him!" he cried. "He's come, Papa's come home from the dead again!" He threw open the door and ran to the gate.

"Little John, wait!" Lucy screamed.

"Little John," Arial called, "the letter . . . it's not Papa! Little John, come here!" She ran after him, but he ignored her calls.

From the open doorway Lucy watched in horror.

Little John was at the gate by the time the rider dismounted.

"Papa—" His words hung in the air. Then, yelling hysterically, he began to pound the rider with his fists. "You're not my papa! You're not! You're not!"

She stood there motionless, not knowing what to do. She watched Arial running to the gate—saw her grab the boy's arms and pull him off the bewildered rider. At once Little John threw himself on the ground and sobbed into the earth.

CHAPTER FIVE

A Season of Ponderings

⚍

t the gate, Arial stooped to comfort the sobbing boy. "Didn't you read the letter?" she asked. "Don't you remember Cousin Casey?"

"Sure'n it's the horse, he remembers," their visitor suggested. "He fed it enough meals that summer, that he did."

Little John jumped up. Between sobs, he shouted, "I'll not be feedin' it again!" and ran into the house.

Dashing straight to the parlor, he threw himself face down on the floor. Lucy knelt beside him. "Oh, Son," she pleaded, "don't carry on so. We all miss Papa. But be glad that Cousin Casey's come. He's goin' to help with the farmin' this year. It's too much for you. You're just a boy . . . " She rubbed his shoulder but he would not be quieted.

The sound of the door opening and closing drew her attention away from the distraught boy. Looking up, she saw Arial with Cousin Casey standing between the parlor and the kitchen.

She rose from the floor, crossed the room, and greeted him warmly. Perhaps twenty-seven now, he was even taller than she had remembered him. But his raven hair and rugged face were the same.

She led the way into the kitchen where the two younger girls had taken over the supper preparations. "I reckon you remember the girls," she said, glancing around the kitchen and naming them as she did so.

"I would have known them anywhere, even if they're all grown up," he answered. "And some mighty pretty colleens ye are."

They laughed lightly then, easing the tension of the moment.

Over supper, Arial explained to Casey that she had gone that day to tidy the hilltop cabin for him and Lucy assured him that they expected him to take all his meals with them.

Little John did not join them for supper for he had fallen asleep where he lay, and Lucy gave orders not to wake him. Casey agreed at once, saying, "Aye, he looks about as wearied as a young'un can get, and if ye'll let him rest a day or so, I'll not let him get that tired again."

———————

Casey kept his promise. For the rest of the season, Lucy never again had cause to worry that the boy was wearing himself out.

Day after day, Casey went to the fields, plowing, planting, and cultivating. Little John worked alongside, learning as he did so under Casey's careful instructions. But when the warmer June days arrived, and Anna Marie lamented that Little John never had time to go to the creek anymore, Casey insisted that the boy go the very next afternoon.

He went regularly, several times a week, after that. Swimming with Anna Marie and their friends, Junior, Jessie Mae, and Bertie Broom helped him lay aside the responsibilities that had so suddenly come upon him. It was not without protest that he went, however, for he remembered that Mama had told him he was the man of the house.

Late in June a package from Russell arrived at the mill for Little John. It contained a fiddle and a note suggesting that while Casey was on Dogwood Creek he might be willing to help Little John learn to play. The boy was clearly pleased with the idea and, at Casey's suggestion, began that very evening to spend his nights at the hilltop cabin with Casey.

While Casey admitted he was not the fiddler that Lee William had been, he played most of the same tunes and played them well. The boy had a natural talent matched with determination that kept him practicing night after night. One night as he put it away, he looked at Casey, discouragement written on his face. "I guess it takes a heap o' practice to be a fiddler," he said.

Casey patted his arm. "Aye, it does indeed!"

"My papa, he was a real fiddler."

"I heard him."

Little John looked wistful as he confided in Casey that he hoped that one day he might have his papa's fiddle. Then, as in an afterthought, he asked, "You know about his fiddle?"

"What about it?"

"That his uncle George gave it to him when the family come here from Indiana? That the fiddle come from Ireland?"

"That I know, Little John. And the painting hanging in yer cabin . . . they both belonged to Ian Brean, they did. He was the first Brean to come to America from County Cork. And I'm the last."

"The last?"

"The last of the family from County Cork. There are no more. That's why I brought the other painting when I came."

To Casey's surprise, the boy remembered something of the other painting—even remembered that it was like the one of the Irish grandmother, only different somehow.

"Aye, it's a good memory ye have!" he exclaimed. " 'Tis Ian Brean himself in the painting that I brought. 'Tis a mystery why he would leave it behind when he took the boat to America. But me father always said it was to remind them in County Cork that Ian Brean was waiting for them in America." He paused briefly before concluding, "Something else me father said . . . Ian Brean always wanted the fiddle and the painting of his wife to stay together. Sure'n ye'll be having them both one day, ye will."

———

Dog days of August put an end to the swimming, for the scum was thick on the quiet water. Then on a hot September evening, just after supper, Junior and Bertie Broom came by. Little John rushed out, sure that they were on their way to the creek. But Junior stopped him in the middle of his greeting, saying that they had come to say good-bye.

Little John's heart sank as the older boy explained that his pa's brother down near New Madrid was poorly and needed help. The Brooms' wagon was already packed and they were planning to leave the next morning.

Bertie stood looking at Little John. He didn't notice that Junior went to the front door, and when Bertie told him that her brother wanted to see Anna Marie, Little John could hardly believe it.

"My brother's sweet on Anna Marie," Bertie said shyly. "Vows he'll come back and marry her someday." Little John's eyes widened as she continued, " 'Course your sister's only thirteen now, but you'll see . . . " Her eyes twinkled. Then looking shy once more, she said, "Little John, you've been my best friend for all my life. I ain't never goin' to forget you."

Little John looked away. "Me neither Bertie," he blurted out. Then he ran to the house and fetched Cousin Casey. "Let's go," he said. "I got to practice fiddling."

He sniffled all the way to the hilltop cabin. Finally, as they sat on the steps, he angrily declared, "They're movin' clean out of the country . . . back to New Madrid where they come from."

"And it's angry at Bertie for leavin', ye are?"

Little John stared into the growing twilight, not wanting to look at Casey. "Ever'body leaves!" he declared. "People are all the time leavin'." The thought struck him that Casey, too, might be leaving; he had not considered it before. "I s'pose you'll leave too!" He spoke accusingly and he dared not look at Casey as he waited for his answer.

Casey cleared his throat. He twirled his cap between his hands. "It's just the season I come for, it is. But if you're askin' would I come back, indeed I would."

"You won't!" Little John declared. "Nobody ever comes back!" He slammed his way into the cabin, fell across his bed, and cried himself to sleep.

At the end of the harvest, Casey left. When he said good-bye to Lucy he promised to come back if she needed him. He hugged the boy, telling him that one day soon he would be both a fiddler and a farmer on his own.

Little John returned the embrace, saying that he was obliged to Casey, but he refused to look him in the eye. As he watched Casey ride away on the roan horse, the boy set his jaw stubbornly, and shed not a tear.

———

Two months later, Little John awoke one morning with a vague sense of sadness. Stirring in the semi-darkness, he became aware of two things. Today was his birthday, and the sadness he felt reached clear down to his stomach.

For a year, he had dreaded this day.

He had dreamed last night, not of his papa who had died on his last birthday, but of Grandma MaryAnn lying on her bed barely breathing, and thrusting a paper towards him. In the dream, he had shaken his head violently and tried to run from the paper, which grew larger and larger as he watched. Frozen in place, he tried then to scream, only to discover that his voice, like his feet, was powerless to obey.

Now, recalling the dream, he thought of the real paper for the first time in months. He held no curiosity about what had happened to it, only a faintly remembered dread of its contents.

Slowly he pulled on his clothes and, when he could put it off no longer, went down to the kitchen. At the wash basin on the stand behind the cookstove, he splashed his face with water and, pulling something from the dirty clothes basket, dried himself. The feeling in the pit of his stomach gripped him yet. He donned his jumper and cap and took the milk pail down from its hook. At the door he paused. "Don't wait breakfast, Mama," he said. "I don't feel much like eatin' this mornin.' "

———

Lucy stared silently at the door closing behind Little John and studied on what to do about the boy. She had watched him growing quieter by the day for a week now and she could almost see the dread in his eyes. It had been a cruel blow of fate for Lee William to die on his son's birthday. Likely the boy would never be able to get it out of his mind, even if he tried—which he didn't seem to be doing.

Turning back to her gravy making, she pondered over yet another worry about the boy. Of late he seemed to be taken up with Mitchell Callaway and Lucy had not yet decided if this was good or bad for her son.

I oughta be grateful, she mused, *seein' as how Mitch is 'bout the only person around what can take the boy's mind off his papa. But I can't help feelin' Mitch ain't good for Little John.* She allowed that Russell might have been right to be suspicious of Mitch. But it was too late to worry about it now. Arial had married him last week. Mitch was family now and, for Arial's sake, Lucy would hold her peace.

She couldn't help observing, however, that an eleven-year-old boy needed a good man around and she wasn't at all certain that Mitchell Callaway would ever fit that description.

Better his Uncle Russell, she thought, and then instantly acknowledged the impossibility of it. She shook her head, remembering Russell's recent visit when he had talked of the growing bond that lay comfortably between them. Right here at the kitchen table, he had talked long into the night while she had listened. Without ever speaking directly of marrying, he had examined the future, and then laid to rest the question of it. In his easy honesty he laid out the simple facts— Lucy would die if she had to leave Dogwood Creek; Russell would die if he had to stay. He had gone to the loft then, where he slept on the cot next to the boy, and Lucy had gone to her own bed pondering over the fact that Russell had never really asked her how she saw the question herself.

Her contemplative mood hung over her through breakfast with the girls. They were halfway through the meal when Little John brought the milk in, took care of it, and went back to the barn, saying that Mitch was walking with him today as he checked his trapline.

After breakfast, Lucy busied herself making bread, brooding over the boy all the while. She measured the salt, sugar, and drippings into hot water and mixed it. After beating in some flour, she added the ferment from its crock on the back of the stove. Again she beat it well, covered it, and set it in the warming oven to work. When she had washed up the dishes and stacked them back on the table, she set some beans to soak for dinner and mixed some gingerbread as a special treat for Little John.

By the time she put the gingerbread in the oven her bread sponge was smelly and puffy, ready for the next step. She added flour until it was stiff enough, then kneaded the dough on its floured surface. As her fingers worked at the task, her mind was preoccupied with visions of the boy growing up too fast with no man around except this one whom she didn't trust.

What's more, she muttered to herself, *there ain't a thing on this earth I kin do 'bout it.*

Fear, mingled with anger, rose in her heart as she worked the dough—lifting, turning, kneading. Gradually the slow rhythmic thud of the movement gave way to a frenzied pounding until, at last, the dough was ready. She slapped it into its iron baking pot and set it in the warming oven for the final rising.

The pot was hardly out of her hand before she grabbed the scrub pail and filled it with hot water. She shaved some lye soap into the water and swished it around so hard that the water lapped over the bucket rim. Making no further effort to coax the suds, she commenced at once to scrub the kitchen floor. For thirty minutes she worked on her hands and knees, attacking every corner with the scrub brush. Satisfied at last that she could find no more dirt on the smooth wooden planks, she mopped up the sudsy water and wrung it into the scrub pail.

When she had pitched the contents out onto the bare winter ground, she put on her cloak and ran to the outhouse, reasoning that it was the only place she could be alone. Once inside, she drew the latch on the door, pulled her apron over her face and burst into tears.

———

In the woods, the boy walked in silence beside Mitchell Callaway. Today, even the company of his tall, handsome brother-in-law could not shake his somber mood. They were crossing the end of Logan Bennett's field when Little John broke the silence. He jerked his head toward the left and asked, "Did Arial ever tell you 'bout the Bennett cave over yonder?"

"Can't say as she has, L.J."

No one but Mitch called the boy by his initials and at the sound of it, Little John always stood a little straighter and squared his shoulders. "Want to see it?" he asked.

Mitch readily agreed and, in response to the boy's request, promised that he would never reveal the location of the cave.

"It's a secret cave," Little John explained, "and nobody knows 'bout it 'cept the Bennetts and us—the Chidesters. But you're part of us now, ain't you?"

"That I am, little buddy," Mitch answered. He threw an arm around the boy's shoulders and Little John smiled for the first time that day.

A few minutes later they peered down into the well-concealed mouth of the unusual cave. Giving a low whistle, Mitch asked if Little John had ever been in the cave. The boy's pleasure was plain to see as he told how that once after the war, his papa had taken him down. "He swung a rope on yonder tree," he explained, "and climbed down. Then he set up a ladder they keep in the cave and helped me climb down the ladder."

"Who's they? Who put the ladder in there?" Mitch asked.

"Pa and Logan Bennett . . . during the rebellion they hid provisions in the cave so if soldiers came through and took what we had, there was food in the cave." Noting the frown on Mitch's face, he asked, "Did I say somethin' wrong?"

Mitch took off his hat and thrust his fingers through his hair before he answered. "No . . . only I don't much like to hear the war called a rebellion."

"That's what Papa always called it. Said he had to go fight in Mr. Lincoln's army to end the rebellion."

"That's one way to look at it, L.J."

When Mitch said nothing further, the boy asked, "What am I s'posed to call it? What do you call it?"

"Well now," Mitch said, looking grim, "I call it 'The War of the Northern Aggression.' But seeing as how your pa fought for Mr. Lincoln's army, your ma would most likely not approve of that. Maybe you could just call it 'The War.' " He gave Little John a friendly slap on the back and urged him to tell him all about the cave.

It seemed to the boy that Mitch had never listened to him so carefully as he did right now. When he had told all he knew about the cave, Mitch asked, "Are you sure nobody else knows about it, L.J.?"

Little John was adamant. His papa had explained to him how it was a secret and Mr. Bennett wanted to keep it that way.

"Well then, we won't tell anyone that you showed it to me," Mitch said. "Not that you did wrong, L.J. Like you said, I'm part of the family now. But we'll just let it be our secret."

Later as they ambled home, the boy grew quiet once more and then asked if Mitch knew what day it was. Mitch nodded, saying that Arial had reminded him that morning.

"I know it's been hard for you without your pa," he added. "I know a man who never had a daddy from the time he was five. His daddy was a preacher . . . went away somewhere to preach and never came back. Got sick and died. Life wasn't easy for him growing up, but he's doing all right by himself these days."

Mitchell seemed lost in thought as the boy studied his face. "Who is he, Mitch? Where's he live?"

"Oh, nobody you'd know, L.J." Then before the boy could press the question, Mitch grabbed him by the shoulder and said, "Speaking of a man, you're going to be one before we know it. You're not the same little kid you were a year ago when . . . that is . . . " He stumbled over the words.

"When Papa died, you mean." The boy finished the thought for him.

———

It came to Little John much later that that had been the first time he had ever said it—that when he was talking to Mitch, he had for the very first time said, "Papa died."

He was standing in the parlor when the thought came to him. The day was over and the evening shadows hung long across the cabin. He had stirred the coals in the fireplace and added a log. In the kitchen the girls and Mama were laying out supper on the table. He could smell fresh-baked bread mixed with the sweet spicy aroma of gingerbread.

He knew the gingerbread had been baked especially for him and there was a sadness in the knowing, a sadness that was different from what he had felt when he awakened. It was a sadness the boy did not fully understand. He only knew it had something to do with being eleven instead of ten, of hearing Mitch openly say he was not the same little kid he had been a year ago, and feeling that it should have made him happy but instead, it made him sad.

He crossed to the window and peered into the darkening evening. For just a moment he stuck his nose to the window and remembered how he had stood there a year ago trying to hold on to the image of his papa. Alone in the darkness of the room, he acknowledged, once again, that Papa was dead and never coming back and that only little boys look for roan horses to come carrying papas home from the dead. Having said it, he felt again the sadness he could not put a name to, knowing only that it had to do both with papas and little boys who went away.

CHAPTER SIX

Little John's Question

In mid-December, winter struck St. Louis and the great river that gave it life. Chilling winds hovered over the Mississippi while great cakes of ice heaved about, damaging or destroying all vessels that used the waterway. Refusing to venture into the water, the ferries hugged the shore and allowed trainloads of freight delivered to the river's edge to lay piled for a calmer day.

The work on Mr. Eads's bridge ground down. The men never quit working but they made slow progress. While all of this was a great inconvenience to Mr. Eads, it provided an unexpected opportunity for his employee, Russell Chidester, to spend some time on Dogwood Creek.

The week before Christmas Russell caught the mail coach to the creek, taking with him a generous supply of commodities for his late brother's family. There were new books for Little John, a supply of flour, coffee, and sugar, and a quantity of hard Christmas candy. In addition, with the help of his landlady, he had purchased goods for Lucy and the girls for their dressmaking. The woman had also persuaded him to include some new Butterick paper patterns. Russell had argued that Lucy had always made the family's clothes "out of her head" and might think him rude for suggesting she needed the newfangled ready-made patterns. But in the end the landlady convinced him that every woman likes to try something new.

It was midafternoon of the second day when the stage came to Carrick's Mill. Grateful to leave his cramped coach, Russell alighted and stretched his legs. There had not been many passengers—only one other, and he had gotten off at St. Clair. Still there was never enough room inside a coach for Russell's stocky frame. The few stops had been hurried, just long enough to change horses and there had been little opportunity to stretch.

He stomped his feet to coax away the chill of the December day as he made his way inside the store.

"Mr. Chidester, what a surprise!" Mrs. Carrick greeted him. "I didn't know you was expected today."

"I'm not," Russell answered, smiling. "Didn't know I was coming until three days ago."

Seeing Old Man Carrick behind the counter, Russell stepped over and offered his hand in greeting. "I have some things to take to the cabin," he said. "I'd be obliged if we could unload them here and leave them until I fetch the wagon."

"I 'spect that Logan can carry you and your provisions," Carrick suggested. He jerked his head toward the cast-iron stove in the center of the store, where Logan Bennett sat warming himself. "I'll go help the driver unload your bundles onto Logan's wagon," he concluded.

"I'm obliged, Mr. Carrick." Russell crossed the room to where Logan sat.

"You're just in time," the older man said. "I'm going your way directly." They shook hands as he added, "I'm glad to see you, Russell."

Before Russell could respond, Mrs. Carrick called, "I just gave Logan a letter to deliver to your niece."

"My niece?" Russell asked curiously.

Nodding, Mrs. Carrick explained, "For Anna Marie. Reckon it's from New Madrid."

He took the letter from Logan's outstretched hand and, after placing it in his pocket, started working his coat off. It was an awkward process with only one good arm but he was well practiced, and his coat had the less common raglan sleeves that allowed more freedom of movement. With his good right hand he pulled the garment off his left shoulder first. When it had fallen halfway to his elbow, he jerked it off his right shoulder and let the coat fall free. Next he slipped out of the right sleeve and, with one final tug, eased the coat from his useless left limb.

He was conscious of Logan Bennett's eyes upon him through the procedure. As Russell hung his coat on the chair, Logan cleared his throat and asked about the weather in the city.

Twenty minutes later Logan suggested they should be going. Once again Russell felt the older man's eyes upon him as he went through the movements, donning his coat. This time, their eyes met momentarily and Logan's face flushed as silence hung between them. Russell looked at him evenly and said, "They tell me that a one-armed Count named Raglan invented these sleeves."

They were seated on the wagon, heading to the road before either spoke again. Then, stumbling awkwardly over his

61

words, Logan began, "Russell, it was wrong of me to stare. Fact is, seein' you put your coat on put me in mind of your mama. Don't seem the same around here without her."

Russell looked at Logan, waiting for the man to explain himself.

"Well, like I said, it made me think of your mama—think of somethin' she used to say, that is."

"Something she used to say?" Russell urged Logan to continue.

"Yep. She always said that you could do anythin' with one arm that other men did with two arms." Pausing only briefly, Logan asked, "I've been wondering. Would you ever come back to Dogwood Creek to stay?"

Russell pondered on the meaning of the question, put as it was with the observation about his abilities. He stared straight ahead, making no attempt to answer.

"It's none of my business," Logan said at last. "Forget I asked."

"It's not that," Russell answered. "You've been mighty good to the Chidesters. I expect you have the right to ask a question now and then. Fact is, I was studying on why you asked it. Sometimes I worry that the neighbors have too much responsibility for my family . . . that maybe they think I should come here and take more . . . "

"Now, you look here, Russell," Logan interrupted, "that's what neighbors are for. If I ask, 'Are you coming back to Dogwood Creek?' it's because I'd like to see more of you. It's got nothin' to do with responsibility. Besides, I reckon ever'body knows how you're takin' care of your brother's family." He jerked his head around and eyed Russell's sacks and packages in the wagon bed.

Russell studied the man carefully, smiled, and said, "Thank you for that. I figured all along that the best way I could help the family was to keep my job and provide money and supplies as needed. I'm glad you understand that."

Their conversation was easy for the rest of the ride as they discussed the growing cold and the work on Mr. Eads's bridge.

As they pulled into the lane at the cabin, Logan remarked, "They'll be surprised to see you."

"Likely they will," Russell agreed. "On the other hand, they never really know when I'm coming. I don't know in time to write ahead. Most of the time I can only stay a day or two, but with the Mississippi so clogged with ice cakes, the work on the bridge will be slow for a while. I intend to stay until the weather clears. Give me a chance to help Little John with his studies and catch up with things that need to be done."

The family's surprise at seeing Russell was no greater than Russell's own surprise at Little John's progress. Not only did he show himself ready for the new reader Russell had brought, but he also played through "Soldier's Joy" with only a few mistakes.

"One day, you'll play just like your papa did," Russell told the boy, "if you keep practicing."

Little John looked pleased and said that he practiced almost every evening. "I go in the back bedroom after supper so's not to bother Mama and the girls."

"That's good," Russell encouraged. "You keep it up."

But that evening, after supper, Little John lingered in the kitchen, taking more time than necessary for his evening chores. The girls had cleared the table and were washing the dishes. Russell and Lucy sat at the table visiting. Russell watched the boy plodding back and forth between the woodpile outside and the box behind the stove and pondered on how his nephew had had more than his share of responsibility for the past year.

A look of exasperation crossed Lucy's face as she asked, "Did you hear a word I said, Russell?"

"Oh . . . sorry. Of course I heard. You were telling me about Arial's marriage."

"They waited almost a year," she said. "I wasn't that easy 'bout it, but wasn't much I could do. Their minds was made up."

"I'm sure you're right, Lucy. Let's just hope everything works out for them."

Russell had not seen Little John come near them. The boy stood there now, a stick of kindling in his hand. "I'm glad they got married," he said enthusiastically. "Now I got me a big brother. Mitch is all the time tellin' me that I'm his buddy."

Lucy smiled halfheartedly at him. "So you've said. Now, s'pose you can find where that kindling goes?" When he crossed the room on his errand, she turned to Russell and asked if he had seen Mitch at Carrick's Mill that day.

"No, I'm sure he wasn't around. He still working there?"

Lucy nodded. "When he's not off on some other job . . . only we don't have any idea what other job he might be doin'."

Russell raised an eyebrow but did not question her. Instead he looked at Anna Marie. "Speaking of Carrick's Mill, I almost forgot. I have a letter for you. It's there in my coat pocket. You can get it, if you like."

Anna Marie dropped the dishtowel and rushed to where the coats hung behind the stove. "Oh thank you, Uncle Russell," she said, clasping the letter in her hand.

"I declare you're blushing, Anna Marie," he teased.

"Probably from Junior Broom," Little John grunted. "She's sweet on him." Having put away the kindling, he had seated himself beside his uncle now.

The question on Russell's face prompted Lucy to explain that the Brooms had moved away at the end of the summer and that she had forgotten to tell him on his last visit. Russell then turned to Little John and expressed his surprise that the boy hadn't written him about his friends leaving.

The boy shrugged.

"Must have been hard, having them move away," Russell persisted.

"Ever'body leaves," the boy answered shortly. He refused to look at Russell. Then, scraping his chair noisily, he left the room. In a few minutes he could be heard sawing away on his fiddle.

In the kitchen, Lucy made excuses for the boy's behavior.

"Pay him no mind, Russell. He never really looks at anybody anymore—leastways not straight on."

———

A week later as he and the boy were doing the early morning milking, Russell brought up the subject of the Brooms once more.

"Little John, do you know it was right here in this very barn where I first saw the Brooms—hiding from the feds, nearly frozen and half starved." He sighed. "It was a long time ago. They've been good neighbors. I'm sorry they're gone."

"I reckon one of 'em will be back, someday," Little John replied.

"Oh?"

"Junior will come back. Him and Anna Marie will get married soon as they're old enough. Way I figure it, he'll come back for her and then she'll go away, too . . . down to New Madrid. Bertie told me."

"Does Bertie write to you?"

The boy shook his head. "No. She could, but she don't." He stared toward the hayloft. "Letters are all right. But when you got a friend, it's better if you don't have to write . . . it's better if people stay . . . " He said no more, but gave close attention to his milking.

Russell had the uneasy feeling that the boy wasn't saying all that was on his mind. "Something bothering you, Son?" he asked. "I mean, something besides the fact that your friends moved away?"

"No, sir."

"Then, why are you so quiet?"

"I was just thinkin'."

"Well now, you've always told me what was on your mind. Want to tell me what you're thinking?"

The boy blurted out his question then, as his cheeks turned a deep scarlet. "Uncle Russell, would you ever want to marry my mama?"

Russell's milk pail clattered to the barn floor and he scooped it up just in time to avoid losing all the contents. The cow switched her tail nervously while Russell righted himself on the stool once more.

"Like I said, Little John. You've always spoken what's on your mind. How long have you been studying on that question?"

"Don't rightly know. But I been watchin' you with her."

Russell had a sudden vision of being scrutinized every time he talked to Lucy. He squirmed on the milk stool. Making an effort to ignore his rising discomfort, he asked, "Why would you want to do that—to watch me and your mama?"

The boy made no response. Russell sat quietly for a minute. He let the cow's bag hang while he reached his good arm across his chest and grasped his withered arm in his hand. He massaged it firmly as he stared at the pail of milk.

"Your arm hurt, Uncle Russell?"

"What's that?"

"Your arm—does it hurt?"

Russell stopped massaging the useless limb at once and commenced milking again. "No, Son. No, it never hurts."

"Then why're you doin' that?"

"Just an old habit—almost forgot about it." Then, smiling, he added, "Used to drive your grandma MaryAnn crazy when I did that."

They sat silently for a few minutes and then Little John looked at his uncle evenly. "You didn't answer my question, Uncle Russell."

"Are you thinking you'd like me to be your papa, Little John?"

Little John squirted a stream of milk into his pail and bit his lip, but he said nothing.

"Sometimes a boy can miss his papa so much that he imagines a lot of things, Little John. Nothing would make

67

me prouder than to be a papa to you. But your mama and me—well, it would never work."

"But I thought you liked her!" The boy's face colored once more as he protested.

Russell drew a long breath. "It's got nothing to do with how I feel about your mama, Little John. She's a fine woman. Don't ever expect I'll meet a finer one. They don't come any better."

The boy waited, as if sensing that there was something else his uncle wanted to say.

"At first, when your papa and mama got married, I resented your mama. You see, Little John, your papa and I—well, we did everything together. I had two little brothers before your papa was born and they died with the fever. So when your papa came along, I sort of claimed him. We never had secrets from one another. He was the best friend I ever had. When they got married, I was afraid your mama would change all that. But she never did. She never let me feel like I was intruding. It was like we all belonged together. So I guess in a way I've loved your mama for a long time."

"Then why don't you marry her?"

"What makes you think she wants to marry me, Little John?"

"Have you asked her?"

"You're a mighty persistent lad, aren't you?"

"Have you?"

"No, Son, I haven't." Russell looked him square in the eye. The boy turned his head at once and clenched his jaw.

"Your mama wouldn't like the city," Russell tried to explain. "I'd never ask her to leave Dogwood Creek. For some reason she's happy here. Probably reminds her of her home in the hills of Tennessee. She's at home here. She'd die in the city."

"Then why can't you come back to Dogwood Creek and live?"

Russell admitted that he had thought about the possibility a lot in the past few months. Little John's eyes widened hopefully.

"Truth is, Son, I couldn't fit into any world but the one I know. I tried it before. I tried for years to prove to your grandma MaryAnn that I could do everything on the farm that any man with two good arms could do. But it was hard. And I hated what I was doing. I was angry at everybody around me. I could never go back to that."

He looked at the boy, his face scrunched as though he were about to cry. The barn was quiet except for the cows swishing their tails and chewing hay from their mangers.

"Little John?" Russell gently broke the silence.

"Yes, sir?"

"You're just eleven years old a few weeks ago. That's pretty young for all the responsibilities you have. I want you to promise me that you will always write to me whenever you need anything."

"Yes, sir."

"And I think you ought to know there's one thing you don't have to worry about because it's not your responsibility."

"Yes, sir?"

"You don't have to find a husband for your mama."

Little John squirmed on his stool and stared at the stall beneath the cow. Then, the flush of color deepening in his cheeks, he mumbled, "I reckon I been actin' like a little kid."

Russell shook his head in quick denial. He reminded the boy that this was the last day of 1869 and that somewhere in the last twelve months Little John had grown up considerably. He reached over and squeezed the boy's shoulder as he added, "One more thing, Son."

"Yes, sir?"

"Even if it's not your responsibility, I thank you for asking. I'm pleased that you did."

CHAPTER SEVEN

Big Brother

~~~

January, 1874

The sun was not yet in its midmorning position when Lucy laid aside her morning chores and took up her quilting at a frame hung from the parlor ceiling. The cabin smelled of winter. Accumulated odors of past meals mingled with the scents of wood burning in the fireplace and rabbit stew bubbling on the cookstove.

The windows steamed over in the kitchen, but from where Lucy sat, she could see clearly through the parlor window. A new fallen snow covered the landscape. As yet, it clung to the bare limbs of the walnut tree, for there was neither warmth nor wind to fell it to the whitened ground below.

Guiding her needle expertly along the pattern, Lucy contemplated the changes that had come in the five years since her husband's death—changes in the family and changes in Lucy herself.

Two years after Lee William died, Lucy's pa, Jubal Tate, had come home from his timber work ailing in his lungs. Before the month was out, he was in his bury hole at the graveyard next to the schoolhouse.

Of her children, only Little John remained with Lucy now. Amy had married a nephew of Old Man Carrick and moved

71

over the county line. May before last, on her sixteenth birthday, Anna Marie had married Junior Broom—he went by Jake now—and Arial and Mitch still lived in the hilltop cabin.

In a sense, Lucy had also moved away and a different Lucy had come to take her place. While she still spoke with the mountain dialect of her heritage, she had lost some of the softness. Finding it necessary to take charge, she also found it necessary to speak her mind—something she had been unaccustomed to doing.

So long as MaryAnn and Lee William were alive, Lucy had depended on them to take charge of things. She couldn't remember having consciously chosen this arrangement, but it had evolved early in her marriage. What Lee William couldn't solve, MaryAnn had always taken care of and Lucy had gone contentedly through the years, removed from the decisions that confronted her husband and his mama.

Losing them both at once necessitated some adjustments on Lucy's part. During the first months, her mourning had been mingled with hard decision-making. She was reluctant to assume such responsibility, but Russell had assured her that she could do whatever she had to do. She hadn't really believed him, but she had tried to practice his advice—"take it one step at a time, Lucy."

It had become easier over the years and in the process Lucy had become more independent. The change had not gone unnoticed. Six months ago, on his last visit, Russell had said to her, "Lucy, you're beginning to act just like my mama." There had been both surprise and approval in his voice. She had not denied the comparison, but had offered an explanation. "All women act alike when they're trying to survive."

She smiled, remembering the moment. He had accused her of becoming independent and she had laughed with him but had reminded him that she was far from independent. It was then that she had told Russell that she could never have managed without his help. Knowing that he was there—that he had insisted that Little John write him at once if there was a need—had made all the difference for her these past five years. Russell had listened intently, his piercing eyes gazing into her own. He had reached across the table and patted her hand lightly, saying, "I want to help, Lucy," and then abruptly rose and left the room.

There had been times when Russell's help was all that kept them going—like the time the mules died. According to the St. Louis papers that Little John read to Lucy, a horse sickness had spread through the country. As healthy animals became scarce, the price of good teams shot up, but somehow Russell managed to find a well-matched team to replace the dead mules.

She shook her head in wonder as she had done a dozen times or more thinking about the new team. Last summer—the summer of '73—the papers had been full of news of a great depression, brought on in part by the loss of horse-power. Nearly a fourth of all horses in the country had died and everywhere work slowed down. But on Dogwood Creek, Little John had plowed with a healthy new team. And in St. Louis, work on Mr. Eads's bridge had continued. So long as it continued Russell would have work. So long as he worked, Lucy knew she could count on him for help.

If it had been for herself alone, she might not have taken his help so easily. But from the beginning she had known it was for the boy. On that first night after Lee William's burying, Russell had read the paper to her—the one she had found clutched in MaryAnn's hand. It was then that he had said to her, "You must let me help you, Lucy. Otherwise you may never be able to give this to him when the time comes." She had seen at once that he was right and the matter was settled. Still she had protested when he bought the new team.

She lay down her needle and gazed at the fireplace, recalling how they had been standing there when she asked him, "How can I let you do this, Russell? It must take a heap of money to buy a team like that."

He had gripped her by one shoulder and looked her straight in the eye. "Little John has enough to worry about with the farm," he said. "Let me worry about buying horses."

When she tried to protest, he had silenced her by laying his forefinger on her mouth. Then, glancing at great-great-grandmother Brean's painting he had reminded her, "Remember our agreement, Lucy."

Now, unconsciously, Lucy rubbed her finger lightly across her lips as she gazed at the painting again.

The clear call of a cardinal broke into her thoughts and she glanced through the window in time to see the scarlet bird flying to the bare lilac bush. She caught her breath at its beauty and smiled as the touch of its tiny feet caused a light sifting of snow to fall away. Fascinated, she watched until the bird took flight once more.

Turning back to her quilting, she breathed a prayer of thanks to God Almighty that they had been able to hang on to the farm. Russell had managed to find someone to help Little John each season with the planting and harvesting. After Cousin Casey, there had been Old Man Carrick's nephew. He had come for two summers from the next county over and then he and Amy had married. Since that time,

Little John had managed with occasional help from Carrick's freed men.

She paused to look at her handwork. Her tiny even stitches, never fewer than ten per inch, had gained her the reputation of an expert quilter. Blue blocks cut from cast-off dresses were joined to white blocks, forming an Irish chain design. Modestly pleased with the effect, she nodded in satisfaction. "Anna Marie will like it, I think."

Thinking about the marriages of her two younger daughters always brought a smile to Lucy's face. But she had never felt easy about Arial's marriage. More than once she had recalled Russell's observation that Mitch was not good husband material for Arial. *He was right,* she mused. Once she had expressed her own doubts to Arial. She sighed deeply, remembering the occasion. Arial had declared she couldn't imagine living without Mitch.

You might say, she's lived without him anyway, Lucy thought. *In the four years they've been married, he's been gone more than he's been home. And Arial's so peaked all the time, a body wonders if she's unwell.*

It was more than Arial's physical condition that made Lucy uneasy about Mitch. She worried about his influence on Little John. She had hoped that the boy would outgrow his childish admiration of the man, but he hadn't. If anything, his fascination with Mitchell Callaway had reached a new intensity. He seemed bound to agree with anything Mitch said. Lucy had found, much to her dismay, that she could not reason with Little John on the subject of Mitchell Callaway. *In some ways Little John's just like Arial. Likely he thinks he could hardly live without Mitch.*

She had seen Little John looking enviously at his handsome brother-in-law more than once. On one occasion, she saw him studying himself in the aged mirror that hung in the corner of the kitchen. He had run his fingers along his angular face and then smoothed back his raven-black hair. She had stepped back so that he would not see her and shamelessly continued to watch as he teased the corners of his mouth into a half smile and jammed his forefinger into the center of his chin.

The telltale gesture had saddened her.

Still wantin' to look like Mitch, she thought. She had pondered what she would like to tell the boy. *Can't he see he's got the Brean good looks from his grandma MaryAnn's family? Before long he'll look just like Casey Brean looked the first time the family laid eyes on him—as handsome a man as a body would ever want to see.* But of course, she could not speak. She dared not let on that she had spied on him in his own private ponderings.

A month past fifteen, Little John already stood nearly six feet tall. Lucy allowed he had a year or so to wait for full height. On the other hand, he lacked nothing in muscles. Five summers of plowing fields and five seasons of chopping wood had produced strong shoulders and well-developed biceps. Lucy reminded him often, "You've got the Chidester build, and all the Chidester men are tall. But you've the face and hair of the Brean side of your papa's family. You're a right handsome young man."

Usually he made little response, but once he had stretched his lanky frame a bit taller and flashed a great smile at her and said, "I reckon mamas always think their sons are handsome."

That was the same day he had asked her if she thought Uncle Russell would ever sell the farm. "What farm?" she had asked. Looking somewhat bewildered the boy had answered, "Why this one. Papa always said Grandma Mary-Ann owned most of this farm and I reckon with her gone, Uncle Russell owns it now."

She had mumbled something like "nobody's going to sell this farm" and let the matter drop. Later, when she told Russell of the conversation, he had said, "I'll not lie to him Lucy, but if we can avoid it, it's best to wait until . . . it's best to do things as Mama wanted."

Coming to the end of her thread, Lucy knotted it close to the fabric, pulled the knot carefully through and snipped the end. As she pulled off a new length of thread, her eyes fell on the shelf that held Grandpa Chidester's schoolbooks. *Little John has done mighty well,* she reflected as she threaded her needle. She knotted the thread once more and pulled the knot through the cloth before making the first stitch.

Little John had laid aside his schoolbooks at last, having satisfied his uncle that he had gone far enough. But he still read and Russell kept him in books. When he wasn't reading he was fiddling. *He'll be as good as his pa one day soon,* Lucy observed.

Lucy wished that Casey or Russell could be around Little John more. She appreciated that both men wrote to the boy. But she reasoned that a young boy needs a good man around to help him grow up right. *If they was here, maybe Little John wouldn't be tryin' all the time to be just like Mitchell Callaway.*

Even in her private thoughts, Lucy had to admit that she couldn't name anything Mitchell did that was wrong. *But I do worry about the way the man thinks,* she always concluded. *Never seems to make much to do about right and wrong. He's all the time excusin' wrong that others do—especially the James gang. And Little John's beginnin' to think just like him.*

So deep in her brooding was she that she did not hear the door open. Only when it closed noisily did she look up.

"Hi, Mama," Little John greeted her. "Mitch come from Carrick's Mill with me." He set a can of kerosene in the corner. "We'll have lamplight for a spell now." He deposited his tote bag on the table and withdrew a newspaper from it. " . . . got ever'thin' on your list this week, Mama." After hanging his jumper on the peg, he spread out the paper and sat at the table to read it.

Quickly Lucy tucked her needle into the quilt for safekeeping, placed her thimble, thread, and scissors on top of the quilt and, with one pull of a rope, raised the frame to the ceiling. Having moved it out of the way, she joined the young men in the kitchen.

Mitch stood in the corner by the window reading. Lucy recognized the look of his paper. It was a special report from the St. Louis Dispatch on the Jesse James and Cole Younger Gang. *He's been carryin' that paper for two months now and must have read it a hundred times already,* she thought.

She met his glance and asked evenly, "Reading 'The Terrible Quintette' again?" To herself she acknowledged that although he had told her the title of the piece, he didn't find anything terrible about the outlaw gang.

Mitch nodded. "I'll wager these men have the fastest horses in the country," he said.

"Beats me how outlaws can keep their horses while the rest of the country comes close to a halt for lack of healthy animals," Lucy replied.

"Well now, I still got my horse." He laughed and then, more soberly, added, "Anyway I wouldn't exactly call them outlaws."

"They rob, they kill. The way I see it that makes them outlaws," Lucy declared, sounding exactly like her late mother-in-law.

"What Mitch means," Little John interjected, "is the James gang only rob from the rich and only kill when someone tries to kill them."

"What are you saying, Little John—that makes their outlawing right?"

"Well, ma'am," Mitch offered, "it does make them different. Besides, like Mr. Edwards says here, Missouri should be proud of the James gang. We're lucky to have men who are so fearless and strong and intelligent."

"I don't much care what Mr. Edwards says," Lucy retorted stubbornly. "I don't reckon you can make somethin' good out of what's bad. And robbin' and killin'—anybody who can think straight knows that's bad." She looked at Little John out of the corner of her eye, hoping to see some hint of agreement.

But Little John was absorbed in his newspaper and paying little attention to the conversation. He looked up, pointing to the paper. "Here's something about Mr. Eads's bridge," he said. "They aim to have it done by Independence Day. No use to expect Uncle Russell until it's done . . . " He paused as he scanned another item. Then, giving a low whistle, he continued, "Look here, Mitch, a letter from Jesse James."

At this announcement, Mitchell lay down the old paper and listened as Little John read the contents of the letter. In a defensive statement, the outlaw denied having had anything to do with a train robbery in Iowa in July of '73.

"So now the robber writes to the St. Louis papers, does he?" Lucy remarked, when he had finished.

"He probably writes there because Mr. Edwards is the only editor he can trust," volunteered Mitchell. "Mr. Edwards used to be with the Kansas City paper but he's moved to St. Louis."

"Maybe Mr. Edwards writes the letters himself," Lucy answered shortly.

Mitchell ignored the comment and once again defended the James boys. "We really should try to remember that Jesse's not had a very easy life. His pa was a preacher and up and left the family behind to preach to the miners out west and never came back—died somewhere in California. Jesse was only five years old. He had to grow up without a pa, and the whole family had a hard time in the war . . . Union regulators chased them around . . ."

"What cause do you have for defendin' outlaws anyway? And since when does growin' up without a pa make it right to break the law?" Lucy's tone was sharp as she interrupted her son-in-law. "I declare, Mitchell Callaway, you talk like they're friends of yours."

He gazed at her, an intense but inscrutable look in his eyes; when he answered, he merely repeated, "He never bothers the poor."

"Well, I should find that comfortin' seein' as how most of the time we're about as poor as people get. But somehow I don't hanker to see him in these parts . . . poor or not." Lucy bit her lip as she suddenly realized that she was acting quite unmannerly to Mitch. After all, he was Arial's husband, and at this moment, a guest in her house. *I should be ashamed,* she thought to herself. Then, mentally defending her actions, she vowed, *I won't have him makin' Little John into an*

outlaw-lovin' man. I won't allow him to do that right before
my very eyes . . . at least not if I can help it.

If Mitch had noticed her sharpness, he gave no indication of it. As he often did, he now flashed one of his most charming smiles at her. "Never you mind. I can take care of the women in this family. Anyway you're all too good looking—nobody'd do you harm."

Plainly, it was useless to continue the conversation.

Anxious to make amends for her lack of manners, Lucy urged Mitch to stay for dinner. "It's almost ready," she declared, "and high time too. It's noon already."

He left soon after they ate and Little John went to the barn to mend some harness, leaving Lucy to return to her reflections. She pondered for a while what she would like to write to Russell, if only she could write. She felt so helpless watching Little John lose sight of what was right and what was wrong. She could accept men seeing things differently—the Chidester men never seemed to hold the same notion about anything, especially about what was going on in the country. She recalled how they had all disagreed about the war in Kansas, and how they had often argued about who was at fault and what should be done. Still they were men with values. Each one of them had respected God Almighty and the holy Book and had tried to do what was right. *Likely, if they was here today, they'd all agree this time. Not one of them would defend a bunch of outlaws. Little John's got a good mind like his pa and his grandpa before him. But right now I worry that it's not enough . . . at least not so long as he's following Mitchell Callaway around.*

81

CHAPTER EIGHT

Mystery

———— ❧ ————

On the next day, as was his custom, Little John headed to the barn before daylight to do the milking. Seeing the stars still hanging low in the sky and appearing closer than usual, he concluded that likely it would be a cold day.

As he opened the barn door, he was greeted by the musty odor of hay mingled with the body heat and breath of the cows and the ranker odor of their droppings. In the shadows of the lantern light he could make out the form of a little screech owl blinking sleepily at him from the rafters above the corn crib. "I'm glad you're still here," he said under his breath. "Better you eat the mice than they eat the corn."

He threw a handful of hay into the manger and positioned himself on the milk stool. Soon a slow, steady stream of warm milk was flowing into the pail.

In the silent surroundings of the barn, he struggled with his conflicting feelings over Mama. He knew it hadn't been easy for her since Papa died, but he wished she would let him be. And he wondered for the hundredth time what she had against Mitch.

More than once he had seen his mama draw herself up straight and tighten her mouth when Mitch was around. *And she clean forgets her manners if anybody says anythin' 'bout the James boys*, he thought. He recalled the many times Mitch had tried to explain to Mama that sometimes a man has to do what he has to do, but of course she never listened.

By the time the milking was over, he had concluded that there were some things women just don't understand—especially mamas. He hung the milk stool on its nail, picked up the lantern and pail, and stepped outside once more.

Just breaking day, he observed as he gazed at the glowing sky beyond the cabin below. The lamplight from the kitchen window and the smoke drifting up from the chimney reminded him that breakfast would be waiting—and by the time breakfast was over Mitch would be at the back door calling for Little John to go check their traplines.

This season, they had set out their traps together. The arrangement particularly suited Little John because it meant that he could be with Mitch almost every morning.

Since they had an equal number of traps, they had agreed to split all the earnings, disregarding which traps yielded the bounty. Uncle Russell received all the hides at his waterfront office and took them to the fur trader two buildings down from his. It was an arrangement Russell had made with Little John the winter that his papa died and there had seemed to be no reason to change it.

Inside the cabin, Little John handed the milk pail to Lucy, threw his wraps over the chair, and sat down to breakfast. As usual, he had hardly swallowed the last of his mush when he heard Mitch's call at the back door. He threw on his outer garments once again and rushed outside. Mitch stood on one foot and then the other, stomping in the snow and rubbing his gloved hands together. His breath steamed in the clear, still atmosphere.

"Thermometer's dropped five degrees," he called, grinning as he spoke.

Little John smiled at the sight. *A little cold never bothers Mitch—fact is, not much does bother him*, he observed as the two of them swung into step and started their trek up the hill.

They walked in companionable silence for a few yards until they came under the great oak tree. There Mitch jerked his head upward and said, "Everybody calls this tree 'The Haunted Oak,' but I don't remember anyone ever saying how it got that name."

"I heard a horsethief was hung on it once," Little John explained. "I don't recollect the whole story, but seems like it was the same man that stole a horse from my grandpa."

"Did your grandpa hang the thief on this tree?"

Little John shook his head. " 'Course not. Chidesters don't go around hanging people."

"Well now, L.J.," Mitch replied, "there's nothing wrong with hanging horse thieves. I'd hang one in a minute if he took my horse." As they passed the barn, he continued, "Now don't tell me you wouldn't do the same if somebody stole Tony."

"Tony's pretty old." Little John chuckled as he answered. "Don't reckon anyone would want him. My pa bought him after the war was over. He's a good enough ridin' horse, but like I said, he's not young anymore."

"Well, just suppose someone stole the team your uncle bought for you," Mitchell persisted. "You'd be ready to hang the thief that took them, wouldn't you?"

Confronted with the thought of losing his team, Little John felt momentarily confused. On the one hand, he wanted to deny the assumption—wanted to say outright that he wouldn't hang a man even if he stole their horses. On the other hand, maybe Mitch was right. Maybe this was one of those times a man should do what he had to do. He stared at the snow-covered ground. Through lips stiffened by the cold, he mumbled, "I'd have to decide that when the time came."

He jerked his muffler up around his nose and mouth and tried to think of how he might change the subject.

"Do you really think my mama's pretty?" he asked abruptly.

Looking somewhat confused, Mitch hesitated for a moment and Little John felt compelled to explain.

"Well, you did say that at the cabin yesterday . . . so I was just wonderin' if you really think she's pretty?"

Mitch hedged. "Don't you think she is?"

Little John enunciated carefully as he spoke through the muffler. "She's kinda old."

"Old!" Mitch scoffed. "Likely she's not more than twelve years older than I am. I don't like to think anybody would call me old in twelve more years."

Little John pondered the possibility of Mitch being old. He had never thought of it before. Somehow he couldn't imagine Mitch looking any different, or being any different than he was right now.

"Your mama's pretty enough, L.J.," Mitch continued. "And anyway, women like to hear you say that even when it's not true."

It was a wonder to Little John how Mitch always said just the right thing to please people—whether or not it was true. He admired Mitch's ability and allowed that it wasn't the same as lying. *He just likes to make people feel good,* Little John thought.

He had to admit, though, that it was hard to determine when to believe Mitch and hard to know how Mitch really felt about him. He wasn't quite sure anymore when Mitch was trying to make him feel good and when he was genuinely praising him. Just yesterday Little John had fired at a rabbit and missed. Even as the rabbit scurried away into the snow-covered bushes, Mitch had bragged on Little John's shooting abilities.

Now, as if he had read Little John's mind, Mitch asked, "How about a little target practice? I'll show you how to hit a moving target, L.J. Watch this!" He raised his sidearm, and held his aim as a cardinal flew between two distant trees. Before Little John could protest, Mitch fired. In horror, Little John watched the explosion of scarlet feathers. With a thud the bird fell, creating a tiny island of crimson blood and feathers on the snowy landscape.

"Now that was a shot, if I do say so myself!" Mitch shouted. He slapped his gun into its holster and thumped Little John's arm, laughing all the while. "Learn to shoot like that and you'll never have to be afraid of a thing, Little Buddy."

Little John stood openmouthed, not saying a word. His stomach felt strange like it had felt every birthday since his papa died. He tried to think what he should say as Mitch thumped him once again. "What do you think, L.J.? Did you ever see anyone shoot like that?" He laughed again.

Little John shook his head as much in wonder as in response to the question. "No, Mitch," he said at last, "never in all my life did I see a man shoot like that." Silently he thought that he would like to shoot as well someday, and then questioned the idea at once, as the feeling in his stomach tightened to a painful knot.

When Mitch and Little John had finished walking the line, they had two skunks and a possum. "We're bound to get a good price on these," Little John said. "And it's about time. Ever'body around seems to be gettin' more money than we got for that first shipment you sent ahead of Christmas." He looked up at Mitch.

"That so?" Mitch's jaw tightened and for a moment Little John wondered if he were angry. He decided against asking and, instead, explained that he had talked to some of the men at Carrick's Mill and they were getting half again as much for each pelt. "That's why I wrote the letter to Uncle Russell asking if there was a better place to sell the hides . . . remember, you took it to the mill to mail it."

Mitch ignored his comments. He smiled his broadest smile, and said, "What do you say, partner, can we head back and get these varmints skinned and stretched on their boards?"

Little John looked at his handsome brother-in-law and, for the hundredth time, envied him that great smile. The idea that such a fine-looking man—a man who was never shy around people— would call him "partner" made Little John feel three feet taller.

With heads bent to ward off the frigid air, they walked in silence for a time, with only the sound of their boots crunching in the snow beneath. When they came to the edge of Logan Bennett's property, Mitch said, "You know, L.J., I've kept your secret about Bennett's cave for a long time. Now I need you to promise me something."

Little John waited for Mitch to explain.

"Promise me you won't go near that cave until I tell you it's okay again."

Little John looked at him curiously. He wanted to ask Mitch why he should make such a promise as that. But something about the set of Mitch's jaw stopped him. Not wanting to break the pleasant feeling of companionship, he nodded his agreement. He felt rewarded when Mitch smiled at him once more and said, "That's my good buddy."

A short while later they came to the hilltop cabin and found Arial watching at the window. She came out at once, drawing her cloak around her as she walked. Little John sucked in his breath at the sight of her. A wrinkled brow emphasized her hollow eyes and unsmiling mouth. Her expression worried him. *Maybe she don't eat right,* he thought. *She don't look like herself anymore.* Arial stood several feet away. "From the smell of things, I'd say you did all right today," she said, wrinkling up her nose as she spoke.

"We did at that!" Mitch replied enthusiastically. He smiled at Arial and said, "You look so pretty, I'd hug you good. But if I did, you'd smell like a skunk, too."

Still unsmiling, Arial held her nose as she leaned over to kiss him lightly on the cheek.

"You goin' on to Carrick's Mill now?" she asked.

"No . . . not today." Turning to Little John, he asked, "Can you skin these out . . . and maybe take care of the traps alone for a few days?"

"I guess so," Little John said, glancing at Arial and back again to Mitch. He refrained from asking why Mitch couldn't check the lines with him. He didn't mind doing the work but it was hard to conceal his disappointment over not having his brother-in-law's company. He kicked his boot into a snow mound and fixed his gaze on the ground.

"Well, I reckon you men have things to talk about," Arial said. "I'll be goin' back to my chores . . . and to my fire. It's cold standin' here." To Little John she added, "Don't be a stranger, now. Come by and see your sister sometime."

"I'll do that. Maybe bring Mama along." As the door shut behind her, Little John turned to Mitch. "I got to be going," he said. "I'll see you soon?"

Mitch hesitated for a moment and then, shaking his head, replied, "Not likely I'll be around until . . . " He stopped as though calculating in his mind. " . . . probably three or four days."

Mitch thrust out his hand. Surprised, Little John offered his own in return.

"Remember now about the cave," Mitch said as he handed over the bounty he carried. He turned on his heel and walked toward the cabin.

———

With both hands full of bounty, Little John made his way across the ridge to their own cabin, wondering all the while at Mitch's curious actions. He reasoned in his mind that mystery seemed to surround Mitch. Most of the time it excited Little John. Now and then he had to admit to himself that it also troubled him but he could not say why.

Fifteen minutes later, Little John deposited the morning's catch at the west wall of the barn. He skinned out the game expertly, carefully ringing each leg at the foot joint, then making the cuts on the underside, and finally working the pelt off the front legs and over the head.

When he had finished stretching the pelts on their boards, he hung them on the barn wall. He could see the sun had almost reached its noonday position, but he wouldn't have needed to check—from the feel of his stomach he knew it had to be dinner time.

At the back door of the cabin he paused long enough to hang his jumper over Mama's clothesline. It would never do to take it into the house. Once inside, he poured water into the basin and carried it to a shelf behind the cookstove.

Shortly afterward, Lucy appeared at the doorway, a change of clothes in her hands. "I smelled you as you came in, Little John. You'll be needing these." She lay the bundle on the table and left him to complete his washing.

Thirty minutes later they sat down to dinner of cornbread and beans. His trapping clothes hung airing on the line and only a faint odor of the morning's catch lingered inside.

"You're mighty quiet, Son," Lucy observed. "Somethin' bothering you?"

"No, ma'am. Just thinkin' 'bout things."

"Deep things, from the looks of that frown."

"Not really." He had in fact been thinking about Mitch shaking hands with him—something he didn't do every day. But he didn't want to talk to her about Mitch. "Been thinkin' about my trappin' for one thing."

"You've been trappin' for almost as long as you've been walking. I've never seen you frown about it before, Little John."

"I know, Mama. Fact is, we've had some prime pelts this year and I reckon they were skinned out good enough. But we're not gettin' the money other folks are gettin'."

"Well, you are splitting with Mitch, Son. Does make a difference."

"I know that, but there's not as much to split as I figure there ought to be. I even wrote to Uncle Russell and asked if he couldn't find another buyer. I figured he'd send a letter on the next stage, but he didn't."

"That doesn't sound like Russell. You sure you sent the letter?"

"Sure I am." He himself had not carried the letter to the mill, but he remembered giving it to Mitch to take. Mitch had, in fact, offered to take it after Little John told him why he was writing to Russell. Little John considered explaining all this to Mama, but she inquired about Arial before he had the chance.

He thought for a moment, recalling Arial's look. "She looks a mite peaked, Mama. Can't explain it exactly, but her face looked . . . well, kinda tired or maybe worried." In an afterthought, he asked, "Do women get that way when they get married?"

"Do you think Anna Marie and Amy look that way?"

He laughed. "Not hardly. Leastways not the last time I saw them. 'Course Arial's been married longer."

"Do you think she looks unhappy, Son?"

Little John was at once sorry he had said anything. Likely if Mama decided Arial was unhappy, she would blame Mitch.

"I wouldn't say that, Mama. Anyway, what could Arial have to be unhappy about being married to a man like Mitch?"

"None of us know about the next person's happiness, Little John . . . or what goes on in someone else's home."

"But Mama, how can you say that? Arial, she tells you everything."

She was not looking at him now. She stared away into the corners of the room. "Not everything, Little John. Anyway, we don't see Arial enough lately for her to tell me very much.

And I reckon she wouldn't say anything to us if she was unhappy with . . . " She left the name unspoken.

Little John wanted to defend Mitch, to remind Mama what a lucky woman Arial was, but he feared it would just end in an argument. Better to keep Mitch's name out of it. "Why wouldn't she tell you? You're her mama."

She looked up at him then. Holding his gaze, she spoke deliberately. "You must remember, she was bent on marrying Mitchell Callaway even when Russell tried to talk her out of it . . . it'd be hard for her to admit that things haven't turned out too good."

"You mean it'd be like admittin' she was wrong?"

"Something like that, Son."

"Well, what if *you're* wrong, Mama?" He could feel a little edge of anger in his own voice, and he couldn't stop it. "What if you're wrong about Mitch?"

She sighed deeply. Little John hated it when she did that. He waited for her to answer.

"I'd be glad if I am, Little John."

Two days later, Little John sat behind the cookstove shelling seed corn. The thermometer had dropped another five degrees and he found it preferable to do indoor chores. In midafternoon a call at the back door announced the arrival of Arial. She let herself in and had just hung up her cloak when Mama entered the room.

"Arial! I'm glad to see you. You'll stay the day, won't you?"

"And the night . . . if that's all right," she replied. "Mitch said it was all right to come if I wanted." She looked at the pile of patching Mama had laid on the table. "If you got a spare needle and thimble, I'll help you patch while we visit, Mama."

She had taken up one of Mama's skirts and was applying a patch to it when Little John asked, "Mitch coming for supper, Arial?"

She pricked her finger then. Quickly she stuck it to her mouth. Without looking at him, she said, "I forgot to mention—Mitch's gone. Took his grubsack and left before sunup yesterday. Likely'll be gone a few days."

Remembering his conversation with Mitch, Little John asked, "Did he say he'd be gone two or three days?"

"Why yes, he did. Why do you ask, Little John?"

"No reason. He said somethin' about it the other day."

Remembering about the cave, Little John asked, "Did he say . . . " He caught himself. Perhaps it would be better not to ask Arial if Mitch had talked to her about the cave.

"Did he say what?" Arial prompted him.

Clearing his throat and stumbling over the words a bit, he asked if Mitch had said where he was going.

"Not exactly. He said something about riding over to Potosi for a few days . . . I don't rightly know. But, no matter, Little John. He'll be back."

She spoke confidently, but the smile had left her face and he saw again that tired worried look of two days ago.

CHAPTER NINE

Suspicions

―――――――――― ∽ ――――――――――

Three days, then four days came and went and Mitchell
Callaway did not come home. When a week had passed,
Little John went to Bennett's cave, not knowing quite
why he went or what he expected to find, but feeling somehow that Mitch's remark about the cave had something to do
with his prolonged absence.

As he approached the area, he stopped abruptly and his
eyes widened in disbelief. Hoofprints circled a nearby tree.
The snow was tamped down as if the animal had been
tethered there for some time. Little John examined the
tracks closely, but could not tell if they belonged to Mitch's
mount. Of one thing he was certain—there had been more
than one horse.

Puzzled, he wondered what it all meant—why would
Mitch ask him to stay away from the cave? And if these prints
belonged to Mitch's horse, why would he bring someone else
here? If he had been here, why would he leave again without
seeing Arial?

The questions tumbled over in his mind as he walked
home. Coming to the barn, he reached a decision. Whatever
it all meant, he was sure that Mitch would not want him to

tell anyone what he had seen. He would just keep it to himself. He was relieved that a light snow had begun to fall. In an hour or so, the tracks near the cave would all be gone.

———————

February was half gone when Arial fetched a little bundle of clothes from the hilltop cabin and settled in with her mama and Little John. Lucy had insisted on it after Logan Bennett brought word that the James gang had held up the train at Gads Hill. "Not safe for you to be alone, with 'em that close," she declared.

Day after day, Little John watched as Arial followed Lucy around like a shadow, trying to give more help than was needed. He could see that his sister's behavior was making Mama crazy. As for Arial—for all her being underfoot, she was so far away in her mind that she never heard a word anyone spoke. More than once he had had to grab her by the arm before he could make himself heard.

He watched the women, seeing the worry in their eyes and not knowing what to say. He kept hoping that Mitch would come soon or, at the least, the weather would change so he could be outside from breaking dawn to setting sun. As it was, he sat behind the cookstove most days, shelling corn, sharpening knives with his whetstone, or making clumsy attempts to mend his shoes.

He pondered over the fact that Mama had been quiet, never once criticizing Mitch—not that Mitch deserved criticism, but he had expected it, had in fact prepared himself to defend Mitch if need be. When it became apparent that no such need would arise, he reluctantly concluded that Mama was more interested in helping Arial in her situation than in deciding who should be blamed for it.

To his surprise, he found himself bringing up the subject of Mitch to Mama. He had not ever intended to do so, but she came upon him one evening as he sat absentmindedly rubbing the palm of his right hand. Only when she inquired whether he had shelled too much corn did he become aware of his movement. "No, Mama, it's not that. I was just rememberin' . . . " He paused and looked around. "Where's Arial?"

Mama had known at once that he did not want to say what he had to say in front of his sister. "She's in the back room," she assured him and, drawing a chair near him, sat down.

He began again. "I was just rememberin' that Mitch shook hands with me the last time we went to the traplines."

"Shook hands? Like he was saying good-bye?"

"That's right. Only I didn't exactly think that at the time. I just thought it was kinda strange . . . the way he acted that day."

He was relieved that Mama only nodded in understanding and said nothing about Mitch. After a time, she lay her hand on his shoulder and said, "We don't know ever'thin' we might want to know right now, Son, but important thing is, we got to help Arial through this." She paused, staring away at nothing in particular. "It's like Russell always says—we got to take it one step at a time."

She left him alone then and they had never talked of it again.

Walking the trapline was the worst part for Little John. He had grown accustomed to Mitch's company in the woods and now they seemed big and quiet and lonesome without him. The mounting supply of pelts only partly compensated for his absence. Little John had sent a shipment of pelts since Mitch went away and would have another full shipment before the season's end.

One grey morning when the smoke from the cabin hovered like a tiny cloud over the roof line, Little John saddled Tony and went to Carrick's Mill for a few supplies. "Looks like we're goin' to have a spell of weather," he told Lucy as he asked for her list. "I'd best go today."

At the mill, he walked into the general store, and at once the men who were gathered around the stove grew quiet. The silence hung there awkwardly until one man greeted Little John and the rest followed his example. Their clumsy attempts at conversation made Little John uncomfortable. He crossed to the counter and handed his list to Old Man Carrick. In return, Carrick handed him a letter from a fur company addressed to Mitchell Callaway and Little John Chidester.

"Mitch usually takes this . . . " Carrick hesitated, his unspoken question written on his face.

"I'll take it this time," Little John replied. He considered the thought that he might be expected to make some explanation for his absent partner, but decided against it. He tore the letter open and nodded in satisfaction at the payment enclosed. Even though Uncle Russell had never answered his letter, he must have found a different buyer. This time they had received a higher payment per pelt. Aware of eyes upon him, he glanced to the group huddled around the stove and announced, "Looks like we got top price for that shipment."

All the men voiced their approval. But their pleasure for him seemed a little exaggerated, their voices a little too loud, and in a moment they all lapsed into silence once more. With growing discomfort, Little John collected his supplies and left the store.

As he stood tying the tote bag behind Tony's saddle, he heard footsteps. Turning, he looked into the sympathetic face of Logan Bennett.

"You and the womenfolk doin' all right, are you?" he asked.

"Yes, sir, we're gettin' along." Little John gave a final hitch to the knot and, facing Logan once more, said, " 'Pears to me like I walked in on something I wasn't s'posed to hear in there."

Logan didn't hesitate. "It's nothin' to be concerned about, Little John. People are sayin' that Mitch Callaway has deserted Arial and they're all concerned for her. Folks around these parts think a lot of the Chidesters. Don't take to some stranger like Callaway walkin' in here and doin' wrong by one of the Chidester daughters."

"I don't like people talkin' 'bout my sister." Anger welled up within Little John as he faced the older man. He felt his face flushing as he spoke.

"No call to worry about that," Logan assured him. "It's not your sister they're talkin' about. They wouldn't do that in front of Carrick anyway, seein' as one of his own relatives married Amy. It's Callaway they talk about. Fact is, they . . . "

Little John studied Logan's face as the older man caught himself. Clearly, Logan had almost blurted something out that he now did not want to say.

Little John prodded. "They . . . ? What was you 'bout to say, Mr. Bennett?"

Bennett shifted his feet and looked at the ground. Then looking Little John straight on he said, "You might as well know, Son. Folks are sayin' that Mitch has some doin's with the James gang."

"If you wasn't such a good neighbor, I'd knock you down!" Little John exclaimed. He glared at the man who had done so much for him and his family.

"Now take it easy, Son," Logan said carefully. "These people are your friends. Not likely they'd make such accusations without reason."

But Little John was already in the saddle. He reigned Tony around and galloped up the road before Logan could tell him what was behind the accusations.

———

For seven days Little John fumed and fought against a growing curiosity over what his neighbor had said.

This morning, he had determined he would talk to Logan—had already walked to the Bennett home and even now stood at the front door.

Cora came to the door in answer to his call. After greeting him warmly, she volunteered, "Logan's at the barn—gettin' his plow in shape."

He made his way to the barn then, contemplating what he would say. He wasn't ready yet to believe that Mitch was an outlaw. Still, he had to hear why the men at the mill would make such an accusation.

"Howdy, Little John!" Logan grinned at him as he looked up from his work. "Plowed your oat field yet?"

"Little wet yet. I'm thinkin' by the weekend I'll start if the weather holds." He cleared his throat before going on. "I reckon I owe you an apology, Mr. Bennett. I come to hear what you got to say." He knew it wasn't necessary to explain what he had come to hear. He leaned against the wall of an empty stall and waited for Logan to begin.

"This ain't easy, Little John."

"Likely, I won't believe it anyway," Little John replied. "But I got to hear why the men feel like they do."

"To tell you the truth, Old Man Carrick has suspected Mitch for a long time. He's been tracking things."

"Tracking things?"

"Yep. Like the times Mitch goes away. Turns out he's almost always gone when the outlaws pull a job somewhere in the state."

Little John's heart rose to his throat, but he forced himself to speak calmly. " 'Most always? But not always? That don't mean nothin'."

"Maybe. Maybe not. But there's more."

Little John feigned more disinterest than he felt and waited for Logan to explain.

"Carrick, he found things missing from the store after Mitchell came. First, he thought it was a mistake, but it happened more'n once."

"What was missing?"

"Money a coupla times. Last time it was food—a big supply of food that a man would carry in a grubsack—only it was enough for two or three men."

"What makes him so sure Mitch took it?"

"For one thing, it disappeared the day before Mitch left Dogwood Creek."

"That still don't mean Mitch took it." Little John was beginning to feel uneasy with the mounting evidence. Still he determined to defend his brother-in-law.

"No, it may not mean that Mitch took it, Son. But Carrick is sure enough about it that he don't aim to have Mitch working there no more—that is, if he ever comes back."

"He'll be back!" Little John spat out the words. "He wouldn't leave Arial that way."

Logan looked at him sympathetically as he replied, "I hope you're right. For Arial's sake, I hope you're right." He paused, stroking his chin thoughtfully. "You may as well know that a lot of people think Mitch married Arial for a cover—that he's using all the Chidesters."

Little John exploded. "No matter what else you think, Mitch loves Arial! What's more, he's the best friend I got!"

"Well now, I would have said your uncle Russell pretty well fits that description."

"Uncle Russell's not here. He left. Papa left. The Brooms left. Casey left . . . " He ranted on, no longer able to control his anger.

"And Mitch didn't?" Without waiting for Little John's response, Logan continued, "I reckon he's stayed around more than the others, but that don't deny the facts, Little John. It's hard to say this, Son, but I got to say it. Carrick has followed the James gang and their plundering and killing . . . "

"They don't kill unless someone tries to kill them!" Little John interrupted. "And they only rob from the rich."

He saw the look of surprise on the older man's face and wished at once that he could take back his words.

"Did Mitch tell you that?"

"What if he did?"

"Sounds to me as if he defended the outlaws considerably."

"Don't mean nothin' even if he did." Little John spoke the words, but deep down he doubted what he said.

Again, Logan looked at him sympathetically. He thrust his hand out and touched Little John lightly on the shoulder. "Whatever comes of all this, we're all your friends. Don't forget that. We all want to do what we can for the Chidester family."

"Yes, sir," Little John mumbled, quieting under the older man's touch.

In a fatherly tone of voice, Logan said, "Ever'body's heard the excuses made for the James gang, Son. But no amount of excusin' has ever made right outta wrong."

Little John knew Logan was right. Still he wondered—did Logan really know the facts about Jesse's family, and if he did, wouldn't he make allowances as Mitch often did?

"You know 'bout the James family?" he asked, looking Logan in the eye.

"Ever'body knows about the James family. Papers are full of the James boys."

"What I mean is, do you know anything about their papa—their real papa?"

Logan looked at the boy curiously. "Hear tell he was a preacher. Left home when Jesse was five or thereabouts. Got sick and died somewhere." Then as if trying to make a deliberate point, the older man added, "There's something else. Jesse's papa helped start some Christian school in Liberty. Back in '66 a gang robbed the Clay County bank there and killed a boy from that very school."

"A gang, you say? Not the James gang?"

"They don't know for sure, but they suspect it was the James boys' first bank robbery." He paused briefly and looked Little John square in the eyes. "The boy just happened to be passin' by the bank when the robbers came out. Strange turn of events, wouldn't you say? The son of the very man who started the college shoots down one of the students in broad daylight? A mighty shame upon a man's good name now, ain't it?"

Little John started to protest, to remind Bennett that if no one knew for sure who had robbed the Clay County bank, that likely James hadn't done it. But he reasoned that he had no need to defend Jesse James.

He pretended indifference. "We agree on one thing, Mr. Bennett. It is a disgrace for a man to bring shame on his papa's good name."

He turned to leave, cutting short any further discussion. "I'm obliged for your time," he said and made his way out of the barn.

As he hurried along, he recounted everything that Logan had said. Reluctantly he admitted the older man was convincing enough to raise suspicions about Mitch. Pain gripped him in the stomach as he wondered aloud whether Mitch had betrayed both him and Arial.

A dim vision of his own papa's face danced before him as Logan's words echoed in his head: " . . . shot down a student from the very school his papa helped start." For reasons he could not explain, this tormented Little John more than all the other evidence Logan had offered.

He was so deep in thought he did not see Arial coming from the hilltop cabin until their paths joined and they were nearly side by side. Startled, he blurted out, "Arial, what are you doin' here?"

"I live up yonder, Little John. Or have I been so long with you and Mama that you've forgotten?"

"No, I haven't forgotten. But I didn't expect you to be traipsin' up there to a cold house." Seeing a bundle in her arms, he reached for it, saying, "Here let me carry that for you. And the next time you need somethin', let me fetch it for you."

"I won't need anything else. I expect Mitch will be home any day. I left him a note. 'Course he'd know where I was anyhow." She smiled mysteriously and babbled on, "He's been home, Little John."

"You saw him?"

"No, but I know he's been there."

He looked at her curiosly, wondering if the separation from her husband was making her crazy.

"I saw fresh tracks at the barn just now . . . like his horse mighta been there last night, but there's no sign of the horse or Mitch anywhere."

He wondered what to say to her. "Probably they was old tracks, Arial," he said at last. He wanted to believe it, but silently he had to admit that Arial knew as much about tracks as he did.

"No, I know they ain't." Then, with a look of hope in her eyes, she suggested, "If you want to check on them . . . "

He handed the bundle back to her. "I'll do that. Won't take long. I'll be home directly."

———

Five minutes later he stood in the empty barn. In all the time Arial and Mitch had been married they had acquired hardly anything. They had never owned a cow and Arial had long ago killed the last of her small flock of chickens. Mostly the barn had been used for Mitch's fine mount. It wasn't hard to see that Arial was right. The tracks were fresh. And very likely they were from Mitch's horse.

He pondered over why Mitch would come home and leave again without seeing Arial. His eyes followed the shaft of light filtering through the open door. Suddenly his heart began to pound underneath his jumper. There in the manger lay a wheatsack knotted in the middle. A paper was thrust into the knot.

The gang entered the bank, wheatsack in hand . . . How many times had he read those very words in the last few years. It was the trademark of the James gang.

Cautiously he lifted the sack and withdrew the paper. *For Arial* was all that the paper said. Angrily he declared out loud, "Arial don't need no outlaw money!"

For a moment he pondered what to do about his discovery. At length, he picked up the sack and thrust it inside his jumper. He wanted to burn the note, but having no fire, he shredded it into fine pieces, walked to the toilet, and threw it away.

Determined not to tell either Mama or Arial, he gathered his composure and practiced what he would say to his sister about the tracks.

She was waiting for him at the kitchen door.

"I reckon you may be right," he announced casually. "Could be fresh tracks. All the same, you'd best stay here, Arial. Mitch will know where to find you."

He went to his loft room then before she could ask any questions.

Once alone, he looked about the room, wondering what to do with the wheatsack. At length he decided on the shelf where his papa's old carpetbag sat. *No one ever looks there,* he observed, thrusting the sack well behind the bag. *It'll be safe until I can talk to Uncle Russell 'bout it.*

CHAPTER TEN

The Wheatsack

————————— ⧈ —————————

Spring burst upon Dogwood Creek with an extravagance unlike anything in its remembered history. Even Cassie Miller, the most talkative old woman on the creek, could not recollect having seen such wild beauty in seasons past. Never had the buttercups appeared in such quantity, nor the johnny-jump-ups so early. Never had the redbud looked so bright, never had the dogwood blanketed the woods so completely.

Even the old men gathered in the store at Carrick's Mill shook their heads in wonder at the season. And Logan Bennett reported to Little John that the tittle tattle about Mitchell Callaway had given way to an endless observation of what beauty could be found on this hill or up that hollow.

April nights were filled with the songs of the laughing frogs and crying toads. In the woods beyond Solomon's Ridge, Little John gathered giant red spongy mushrooms that Lucy soaked overnight and fried for breakfast. Arial, who had hardly stepped beyond the bounds of the chicken house in two months, took long walks in the woods and brought back armloads of dogwood blossoms for decorating the parlor.

On a mild May evening, as the three of them sat down to supper, Lucy recalled, "Your grandma MaryAnn always favored this month." She turned toward the open kitchen door as the call of a bobwhite sounded from the fence row. With a smile, she added, "She would have loved it this year."

Little John allowed that the softness of the season had worked a certain charm on the women. Arial's eyes seemed brighter and she managed to smile more often. Mama seemed pleased enough, but he suspected that she still brooded over Arial's situation.

His suspicions were confirmed one June morning when a letter came from Uncle Russell. He had opened it at Carrick's Mill and read it through. As he hurried out to the garden and waved it in his hand, Lucy looked up from her hoeing. She wiped her face with the corner of her apron. "You fetch a letter from one of the girls?" she asked eagerly.

"No'm. It's from Uncle Russell. He wants us both to come to St. Louis for the big celebration for Mr. Eads's bridge." He read the letter to her as she stood with hands clasped on the top of her hoe.

> *The opening will be celebrated on July 4. It should be a big celebration, one of the biggest St. Louis has ever had. It would make me so happy and proud to have the two of you with me for this grand occasion. Little John can stay with me and I will make arrangements with my landlady for a room for you, Lucy.*

He had closed the letter begging them to consent and promising that he would send the money for travel if only they would come.

The look on Lucy's face told Little John that she was pleased. Still, he was not surprised to hear her say at once, "No, I can't go, Son."

"But—" he started to protest.

"I could never leave Arial at a time like this."

"We could take her. I know the only reason Uncle Russell didn't ask for her to come was that he didn't know that Mitch is gone."

Lucy's eyes widened in surprise. "Didn't you write him about Arial?"

"No, ma'am. What could I write?"

"That Mitchell Callaway has deserted your sister, that's what."

The sharpness of her tone provoked Little John. "We don't know that, Mama." Even as he spoke, he remembered the wheatsack hidden in his room and wondered why he still felt compelled to defend his brother-in-law.

Clearly exasperated with him, Lucy said, "You write Russell that you'll be there." She bent to her hoeing, signaling that the matter was settled.

Little John mailed his answer on the next stage out. He didn't explain why Mama wasn't coming, just that he would come alone. He was glad there was plenty of work to keep him busy for the next three weeks.

On the morning he was to leave, he rose early, dressed hurriedly, and gulped down his breakfast, leaving Mama and Arial still eating while he returned to the loft to gather his things. He struggled with the extra shirts Mama had laid out, trying to fold them just so. He took his spare pair of trousers from the peg on the wall and rolled them up. As he jerked down his papa's old carpetbag from the shelf, the hidden wheatsack fell to the floor.

He was still searching for a new hiding place when he heard footsteps on the stairs. Quickly he thrust the sack under the cornshuck mattress. His heart jumped wildly as he straightened up once more and saw his mama come through the door.

"Can I help you, Little John?" She didn't wait for an answer but went directly to the bed and refolded the shirts and trousers. He looked at her helplessly.

"You ain't had much practice packin' a carpetbag, Son." She smoothed a fold on the last shirt and placed the garments in the bag. "There now. I 'spect that will travel better."

"I'm obliged to you, Mama. I wish you was goin', too."

She smiled, but did not look up. As she buckled the bag, she reminded him, "Mind you, tell Russell I'd be proud to come, 'cept Arial needs me now."

"Yes'm. I'll explain."

He followed her down the stairs where Arial waited to tell him good-bye. He hugged his sister with his free arm. "I'll be back soon," he assured her and immediately worried that the remark might remind her of Mitch, who had never come back at all. Pausing at the door, he kissed Mama lightly. She clung to his arm for a moment and, almost in a whisper, reminded him once more, "Remember to tell Russell for me."

———

As had been arranged by his uncle, Little John arrived in St. Louis on the evening of July 2. They walked the three miles to Russell's rooming house, partly because Russell knew Little John was used to walking and partly because the omnibuses were overcrowded with people who had come to view the great event.

They picked their way through the crowded walkways and, all the while, Little John gaped at the street where wagons and horseback riders vied for space with the omnibuses. Several times he bumped other pedestrians with the carpetbag that he had swung over his shoulder. After the third such incident, Russell explained apologetically that St. Louis was not always so crowded. "If it was, maybe I'd be out at Dogwood Creek for good."

Remembering how his uncle felt about the creek, Little John shot back, "That would take a heap of a crowd, I reckon."

Russell ignored the remark. "Hotels are all full already. Don't know where they'll put people. Likely a lot more will arrive tomorrow. Trains keep dumping them at the docks on the Illinois side and I can't believe how many came in by boat today before I left the office."

"Must be important, this dedication of the bridge, Uncle Russell."

"Important enough. But it's just the way St. Louisans are . . . always ready enough to have a parade. Some say this town's been doing that ever since the French settled it. Of course they're quick to add that they've never had a celebration like this one. It's going to be a real grand Fourth of July."

Little John could see the excitement on his uncle's face as he continued with his description. "You missed the big event. Mr. Eads has been testing the bridge. He held a public test—crowds everywhere. He borrowed fourteen big locomotives, filled them with coal and water and as many passengers as could fit in or on them. Then he crossed the bridge . . . and just kept on crossing it."

Little John's mind already whirled with the sights and sounds all around him. Now he tried to imagine the sight of fourteen locomotives on the bridge that crossed the big river. His eyes widened as he asked, "Did you see it, Uncle Russell?"

"Oh, indeed I did. First he sent seven cars across and they stopped every time they came to one of the arches. Then he sent all fourteen—seven cars on each track. They crossed the bridge beside one another. Afterwards he had them cross in a single line—"

"That's a lot of locomotives," Little John interrupted.

"Not enough to cover the tracks, though. That's what Mr. Eads really wanted to do—fill the bridge with locomotives from one end to the other."

"Why didn't he? Was he afraid it would fall down?"

Russell laughed heartily. "No, not at all. Fact is, he couldn't find any more locomotives to borrow for the test."

It was bedtime when they came to the rooming house, but Little John was too excited to sleep. He lay awake for hours remembering the evening's events and anticipating all that would happen tomorrow.

———

He awoke to a stifling-hot, moisture-laden morning.

"We'll go to my office for a while after breakfast," Russell explained, after wishing Little John good morning. "We probably won't be back until after dark tonight, so you're in for a long day."

Uncle Russell had already been to the kitchen to fetch water for their shaving. He set the pitcher on the washstand and motioned for his nephew to go first.

Little John poured the hot water into the porcelain bowl and lathered his face. Peering into the mirror, he tried to concentrate. He didn't want to cut himself. He wanted to look his best as he made the rounds with his uncle.

As he dressed carefully in the clean trousers and homespun shirt that Mama had prepared for him, it came to him that in all his life he had paid little mind to how his uncle managed so well to groom himself. Fascinated, he watched as the older man shaved and completed his dressing. With his good hand, Russell swiftly buttoned his shirt. Then, from the mirror stand, he pulled a black tie that was formed into a large flat bow. Again, with his one good hand, he quickly pulled the tie over his head, stretching the elastic in the back as he did so. After adjusting the bow at the front, he turned down the collar.

"I never saw a tie like that," Little John observed. "You sure are handy with it."

"Blamed nuisance," Russell muttered. "When I went to work for Mr. Eads, I felt out of place with no tie, but tying a flat bow is one trick I never got the hang of with one hand. I said something about it to my landlady one day. A few hours later she comes to me with this contraption. Said her husband tied it and then she cut the back out and replaced it with elastic. Of course I have to turn the collar down—a lot of men don't—to hide the elastic."

Little John thought for a minute. "She must be a nice landlady."

"Nice enough," Russell replied. His eyes twinkled as he continued, "Of course, she takes a special interest in all the bachelors because she has two daughters she wants to marry off."

"You fixin' to marry one of them?" Little John felt a twinge of alarm as he asked the question.

"Nope. But I appreciate their mama's attention anyway." He laughed shortly and then spoke more soberly. "Don't think I'll ever marry, but if I did . . . well it wouldn't be one of them." He seemed lost in thought for a moment. Then abruptly he waved his hand and said, "If you're ready, we'll go down for breakfast."

———

They seated themselves and almost at once a woman brought their meal. She smiled sweetly at Uncle Russell as she set it before them. He thanked her curtly, and turned his attention to Little John. As the woman walked away, he smiled wryly and remarked, "One of the marriageable daughters."

Little John arched his eyebrows and craned his neck for a better look, but the woman had disappeared into the kitchen.

"Are you having a good time?" Russell asked.

Little John nodded enthusiastically. In the short time he had been there, he had almost forgotten about Mitch and Arial and the wheatsack hidden under his mattress. "I'm obliged to you, Uncle Russell," he said. "I'm glad to be here."

"No, Little John. I'm the one who's obliged. You don't think I'd want to celebrate such an occasion all by myself, do you? And I can't think of anyone I'd rather celebrate with."

"You could have taken one of the marriageable daughters," Little John teased.

Russell wrinkled his nose and rolled his eyes. They laughed easily together. "Won't be long before you're looking for some marriageable daughter," Russell suggested. "I'll scout around for you, if you like." He grinned.

"I've got time. Won't be sixteen until December. Anyway, I got enough to take care of as it is." He looked suddenly sober.

"Don't ever try to do it alone, Son," Russell responded to the boy's serious tone. "I'm working steady, bringing in good money. I aim to see that you're all taken care of . . . I'm sorry your mama wouldn't come."

"She appreciated the invitation, but . . . " Little John hesitated, not wanting to talk about problems just yet.

"No need to explain. I didn't much expect her to come." A hint of anger edged Russell's voice.

Little John pondered the meaning of this as he ate his biscuits and fried eggs. He noticed the frown playing about his uncle's face. The older man seemed to be lost in thought again. He clutched his withered arm momentarily, then, as if remembering his nephew's presence, immediately changed his expression. He drew himself up straight and asked, "Is your mama well?"

"Yes, sir." Little John looked away.

When he said nothing more, Russell said, "You don't sound exactly sure about that somehow." His expression registered concern.

Sure that the mere mention of problems would ruin the special feeling of the day, Little John searched for some way to put off the inevitable conversation. Reluctantly he began. "Mama would have come, but she couldn't leave Arial."

"In the family way, is she?"

"No. I reckon Mama would like that in one way. She'd like having a little one around. On the other hand she's likely glad Arial don't have one considerin' . . . " He paused a moment before blurting out, "Mitch is gone."

"From what I hear he has a habit of disappearing."

"This time it's different."

Russell raised an eyebrow and listened intently.

"He's been gone for almost six months. Ever since the Gads Hill train robbery. Folks on Dogwood Creek think he's hooked up with the James gang."

The older man looked startled at the remark. "What do you think?"

"I don't know what to think no more. Fact is, Mitch disappeared two days before the robbery and he ain't been heard of since." He spoke with more despair than anger.

"Little John, I admit I've never thought Mitch was good husband material for Arial, but I don't think you have anything but a coincidence here. Besides, I thought you trusted Mitch."

"I do!" He shifted uneasily on his chair before adding, "That is, I did . . . I don't know—I'm so mixed up. Logan Bennett told me that Old Man Carrick figured out Mitch has been gone just about ever' time there's been a gang robbery in the state."

Russell let out a low whistle. "Is he sure?"

Little John was quiet for a moment, still hesitant to fully admit his doubts about Mitch. "He gave me a list . . . do you want me to give it to you one by one?"

"That won't be necessary, Son."

Little John saw sympathy in his uncle's eyes and the look brought unwanted tears to his own. He blinked hard and pushed his food around on his plate. When he had regained his composure he volunteered, "There's somethin' else." For fifteen minutes he talked, giving Russell the details of how he had come to find the wheatsack full of money in Arial's barn.

Russell jerked up a little straighter in his chair. "What did Arial do?"

"Arial don't know nothin' 'bout it. I tore up the note and hid the sack. It's home under my bedtick. I want to turn it in somewhere but I don't know where and I'm scared of what they might ask me when I do. I was waitin' for the chance to talk to you."

"You could take it to Potosi to the Sheriff," Russell suggested. They talked about it then, thinking through the best way to handle the matter. Afterward Russell asked, "Did you tell your mama about it?"

Little John shook his head. He played with his food while he admitted that partly he had kept it from Mama because they argued over Mitch a lot. "She don't like Mitch. She's all the time faultin' him."

"And you're all the time defending him?"

Color rose to Little John's face as he admitted that, yes, that had been the case.

"I don't mean to be unkind, Son, but it strikes me that when a man has suspicions of another man and some mighty solid evidence to back up those suspicions, it doesn't make a lot of sense to defend him to others who have the same suspicions. Your mama's a reasonable woman. Maybe you should tell her what you know for sure—about the money anyway. And let her help you decide what to tell Arial." He rose after that, saying, "We need to be going. I have a surprise for you at the wharf and if we don't hurry, we're going to miss it."

———

Back on Dogwood Creek, Lucy went about her chores, daydreaming about what it might have been like to go to St. Louis with Little John. It was early morning and she had made up her mind to tidy up his room before it got too hot in the loft.

Already she had cleaned the lamp globe and replaced it, swept the floor, and dusted the wall shelf. Now she scooped the shuck mattress from the bedstead, intent on carrying it outside to air. Something fell to the floor. When her eyes fixed on the object, a strange fear rose up within her. She stood, momentarily welded to the floor, wondering why the sight of a wheatsack should cause her heart to pound. With great effort she tried to recall where she had heard something about wheatsacks. When it came to her, her heart pounded so hard she felt she might choke. Her thoughts jumbled together. *The newspapers . . . Mitch readin' about the James gang . . . the wheatsack their trademark . . . here under Little John's bed ticking.*

She felt the color drain from her face as she stooped to pick up the sack. She was torn between wanting to know the meaning of it all and not wanting to know anything. About one thing she had little doubt—Mitchell Callaway somehow was involved in this.

Dropping both sack and ticking across the bed, she fell upon it and pushed her face deeper and deeper until her nostrils were filled with the musty odor of corn shucks. There she stifled the sobs that would not be stopped and moaned within herself. *How could I have let this happen? How could I have let Lee William's son grow up to be a common thief?*

CHAPTER ELEVEN

Mr. Eads's Bridge

ittle John stood at the window of Russell's office, gazing at the teeming waterfront. It came to him there that he had never seen so many people before in his lifetime. Pulling out his handkerchief and mopping his face, he allowed that in spite of the heat, St. Louis was almost too exciting to be real.

Fascinated, he watched a boat maneuver its way into the harbor and cough up its passengers onto the wharf. He saw another take on some lumber and a few pigs, but none of the boats were taking on passengers. *Ever'body comin'—nobody leavin',* he mused. So engrossed was he in the waterfront happenings that he did not hear Uncle Russell come to his side. He felt a touch on his shoulder and turned to see the older man there.

"We have to meet a boat," he said. "I can see it coming this very minute. We'd best hurry along."

Little John followed behind as his uncle made a path through the crowded sidewalks. Coming to the waterfront, they broke into an open area and crossed to the foot of a gangplank laid out from an arriving boat. Already passengers were spewing forth, losing themselves among the masses who crowded the cobblestones. Suddenly Russell commanded, "Wait right here. Don't move. I'll be back."

Little John watched as Russell pushed against the moving mass of people. When the back of his head disappeared and Little John could see him no longer, he waited nervously, hoping that his uncle would be able to find him again—that they would not lose each other in the crowd.

When he reappeared, ten minutes later, Little John stared, mouth gaping, not believing what he saw. There, standing tall and handsome beside Russell, was none other than Casey Brean.

He fell into Casey's outstretched arms and then turned and hugged his uncle also. "You said you had a surprise," he declared, "but I never figured on seein' Casey here."

There was little opportunity to visit amidst bumping pedestrians going in all directions, so once more Russell struck out, calling over his shoulder, "Follow me."

Back at the office, Casey and Little John planted themselves in front of a window and talked for an hour while Russell finished his business for the day.

After inquiring about Lucy, Casey reported on George Brean's health. "He's feeling poorly, he is. Hated to leave him, ye understand, but he insisted."

Russell asked Little John once again to explain to Casey why Mama had stayed home with Arial. Casey listened intently, shaking his head periodically and voicing his sympathy for Arial.

At noon, the three walked to a rooming house a short way down the street and ordered dinner. Little John studied the faces of the two men, enjoying the thought of being almost a man himself, and having a holiday with them. *I was wrong to think anythin' could ruin this day,* he thought. *I'll be thinkin' 'bout this clean into harvest time.*

Later, glancing out the window, he saw a long building with a sign, *Donzelot and Sons, Best Prices Paid for Pelts.* The name was familiar—it was the company that had bought his last two shipments. It was on his lips to ask Uncle Russell about the furs, but Russell was out of his chair and moving toward the door. Little John decided to ask him later and followed closely behind.

They spent a long, hot afternoon walking the waterfront and, when evening came, the heat still hung heavy over the city. They stood at the bridge, where hundreds of other visitors had gathered, and gazed at the thing that Mr. Eads had done.

In the lamplight and by a clouded moon, they studied the great arches reaching aross the river. Almost as if he were talking to himself, Russell recounted the many times along the way that Mr. Eads had faced discouragement and opposition.

Little John watched his uncle's face grow serious in the dim light as he recalled that Mr. Eads had never given up. Russell stared off into the murky river below, and said, "Sometimes, I wonder . . . maybe people give up too soon."

Little John had the uncomfortable feeling that Russell was talking about himself. But he could hardly imagine that his uncle had ever really given up on anything important. He wanted to say that, to defend him somehow, but the look on Russell's face silenced him. For a moment he wondered if his uncle had forgotten that he and Casey were there.

They walked home slowly, glancing through open doors into crowded hotel lobbies and nodding to those who sat outside on the steps. They saw wagons parked in every vacant spot to be found, and people sleeping on the ground.

Back at the rooming house, they found the room suffocating even with all the windows open. There was very little breeze to relieve the heat. Still, Little John fell asleep easily.

———

He was still in a deep sleep at dawn when the sounds of guns awakened him. Before he opened his eyes, he heard Casey asking, "What's the guns for?"

"Just part of the celebration," Russell answered. Little John sat up on his bed then and listened sleepily to his uncle's explanation.

"Thirteen shots for the thirteen original colonies. There'll be more, I hear. At nine o'clock they'll take two guns to the east side of the bridge and fire echoing shots with them that are left on the west side. I hear they plan to fire a hundred shots in all. Parade starts after that."

They dressed hurriedly and lost little time over breakfast. By the time the guns began their nine o'clock firing, the three of them were seated on chairs on the balcony of Russell's office. It was crowded with men who had worked on the bridge, all laughing and joking and taking pride in the thing that they had done.

"They say the parade is fifteen miles long," one man commented to Russell.

Little John whistled at the thought.

When it began, he leaned forward, chin in hand, and gazed at the sight of colorful uniforms and unfurling banners stretching out over the streets below. Sounds of tramping feet, the clip, clip, clip of many horses, and music from countless bands, blended together, adding to his excitement over the moment. Each brightly decorated wagon seemed greater than the one before, and Little John's eyes darted from one to the other. Midway through the procession he spotted a large painting of the bridge displayed on the wagon of Bridge, Beach and Company, stove makers. As he strained to get a better look, a fire alarm sounded and the drivers of several fire engines snapped their reins, urging their teams out of the parade line. Amidst the screams of women and children and the squeals of rearing horses, Little John wondered anxiously what might happen. He was relieved shortly to see order restored once more.

His uncle pointed to the triumphal arch. "There's a picture of Mr. Eads on that arch," he said, "and beneath the picture it says, 'The Mississippi discovered by Marquette 1673; spanned by Captain Eads 1874.'"

He drew himself up a bit straighter, stared at the great bridge and smiled thoughtfully, as he added, "Mr. Eads was all the time telling the men that when the bridge was done it would be the toil of many hands."

Casey spoke up then. "Sure'n ye've done your part, Russell. Must be excitin' to be part of such a gr-r-and thing." He rolled his r's in emphasis. "It's glad I am to be here now, but b'gory I could never be happy anywhere but on a farm."

Little John nodded, feeling that Casey had just put into words what he was thinking.

"The Almighty didn't make us all alike," Russell responded with a grin. Drawing their attention to the bridge, he explained that the fancy cars crossing before them were called palace cars and were filled with important people who had come for the celebration.

"They're taking them to the Celebration Pavilion," he added. "Captain Eads is going to make a speech."

They went to the pavilion in time to hear Mr. Eads. Unlike Casey and Russell, Little John was much too distracted by the milling crowds to hear what the great bridge builder had to say. He felt chagrined momentarily as he saw his uncle gazing intently at the speaker, and he hoped that Russell would not ask him any questions about the speech.

Much later in Russell's room, tired and hot, they sat in the twilight and talked over the events of the day. At length, Little John remembered having seen the fur company the day before and asked his uncle about the furs.

Russell confirmed that he had indeed taken the pelts to the very same company Little John had seen. "They seemed mighty pleased with your pelts."

"All three shipments?" Little John questioned, a note of disbelief in his tone.

"Why yes," Russell replied. "Weren't you happy with the payments?"

As they discussed the fur shipments, it became apparent to Little John that his uncle had never received the letter asking him to find another buyer. What's more, according to Russell, Donzelot had bought all three shipments and paid the same price per pelt each time. "Why would you want me to find another buyer?" the older man asked.

"Seemed like ever'body on the creek got a higher price on their pelts than we did for that first shipment, so I asked if you could try somewhere else for us. On the last two shipments I got the same as others so I reckoned you must have found a better place to deal with."

"There must be some mistake, Little John."

"No, we got less the first time. Mitch told me . . . " Little John stopped in sudden realization. *He cheated me. He cheated his own brother-in-law.* Aloud he said, "Mitch, he just brought my half of the payment to me, telling me what we was paid. I never saw the paper. And then I wrote you and asked Mitch to take the letter to Carrick's Mill when he went to work. I reckon that's why you never got the letter."

Russell had arisen from his chair and gone to his desk in the corner. After lighting the lamp, he withdrew several papers from the desk drawer. "Yes, here it is," he said, holding a paper to the light.

Little John came alongside him.

"This is the first shipment, the one before Christmas. See—here's the price per pelt." He pointed to the figure and then, showing a second and third paper, went on. "Now look at this figure, and this one—your last two shipments. It's the same price."

Studying the first figures carefully, Little John let out a low whistle. "That's a heap more than Mitch said we made." He turned his gaze away from the papers.

Russell looked grim. He grabbed his useless limb, massaging it for a moment. "I'm sorry, Son."

Casey, who had remained silent through the conversation, looked sympathetically at Little John. "You've had your share of problems with that Irishman. Makes me sorry thinkin' we've come from the same place, it does." After a pause, Casey continued, "Ye'll be pardonin' me for sayin' so, but I never trusted the man and by all that's holy I knew in my heart that he wouldna bring anythin' but pain to that lovely little colleen of a sister of yours."

They sat in the lamplight then, talking long into the night, with Little John admitting that, for a long time, he had refused to call Mitchell Callaway a common outlaw. "I had doubts, but I tried to find excuses for him, 'cause I never wanted to say that Mitch was plumb wrong. He's different from ever'body else—dresses different, always knew just what to say, never afraid of nothin'."

"Little John, when you're growing up, it's sometimes hard to see what people are really like," Russell said understandingly. "It's easy to want to be like people who seem like they can handle anything."

"Even when you see your own sister changin' into an old woman?" Little John demanded.

"Been hard on Arial, has it?" Casey asked.

"Almost from the beginning. Mama, she worried all along that Arial had some secret troubles. Me, I thought she was unhappy, but I was bound it had nothin' to do with Mitch."

"And how is Arial, now?" Casey asked.

"It's like she's given up. Kinda hard to hold her head up, seein' as how he run out on her and all."

"Your sister's got nothin' to be ashamed of." Casey spat the words out.

"Does she suspect anything?" Russell asked.

"I don't rightly know. She never says nothin'. But Mr. Bennett, he said once he thought Arial's known for a long time that Mitch is connected with the James boys and she just don't want to admit it."

Russell scratched his chin thoughtfully and then suggested that they keep everything about Mitchell Callaway between the three of them until he could do some further checking. "We'll just keep our ears and eyes open for a while," he said. "You still get the St. Louis paper?"

"Ever' week."

"Well, just don't be taken in by Edward's editorials. If a man listened to him, he'd think that the state of Missouri had no finer examples of manhood than the James and Younger bunch."

"Mitch thought Edwards was right."

"He defended the outlaws, did he?" Casey asked, his Irish inflection creeping into the question.

"Sometimes he wouldn't say who he was talkin' 'bout, but I always knew . . . at least I knew within reason he was talkin' 'bout them. Always remindin' me that Jesse grew up without a papa and always sayin' almost in the same breath, 'A man's gotta do what he has to do,' like ever'body kinda makes his own rules . . . within reason."

"You've been taught better than that, Little John!" Russell's tone was sharp for the first time.

"I know. But sometimes . . . well, sometimes I can't figure out how a body knows what's right and wrong no more."

"That's not so hard to figure, Son. The Almighty didn't leave us in the dark. If the Book says flat out something is wrong, you got no cause to call it anything else. If it doesn't . . . well, then you might have to study on things and make up your own mind. But don't ever forget that stealing and murdering is wrong and no amount of fancy talking can change that."

"Mitch was a fancy talker, all right," Little John replied, an edge of anger marking his words. "Do you know he never once called me, 'Little John'? Always called me 'L.J.' or 'Little Buddy.' He said 'L.J.' sounded more like a man and he called me that from the time I was ten years old."

For a moment no one spoke. Then Russell asked, "Would you rather not be called 'Little John'?"

Little John fought back his anger. At length, measuring his words carefully, he said, "If it's all the same, I'd just as soon you'd call me 'Little John.' I don't want to be called nothin' that would remind of a man that cheated me out of my pelt money."

CHAPTER TWELVE

Little John's Secret

———— ❧ ————

Little John stirred in the morning quiet. Coming just to the edge of consciousness, he expected to find himself in the boarding house in St. Louis. But even before he opened his eyes he discounted that possibility, for he remembered the long ride home and how he had thought of little else on the journey but Mitchell Callaway and the trapping money. As he came fully awake, he felt the anger welling up once again.

He knew it was late, for he could smell coffee boiling and meat frying in the kitchen below. Forcing himself to a sitting position, he pulled his clothes from the pile where he had dropped them last night and hastily put them on. As he did so, he resolved that today he would ride to Potosi and return the wheatsack as he and Uncle Russell had discussed. *But I'll not tell Mama yet,* he thought. *I won't talk 'bout Mitch Callaway today—not to Mama, not to Arial, not to nobody.*

Coming into the kitchen, he found Lucy standing before the cookstove stirring the gravy. On the table was a plate of side pork, fried crisp and brown.

"Mornin', Mama," he greeted her.

"Mornin', Son." She hardly looked up. Something about her countenance bothered him. *No sense invitin' trouble*, he thought, deciding against asking any questions.

Then, speaking offhandedly, he said, "I got some business to tend to, Mama. I'll be gone most of the day. Could you fix me a grubsack?" He hoped that she wouldn't pry.

To his surprise, she simply nodded, dipped up the gravy, and set the bowl on the table. After she had set out the biscuits from the oven, she turned away and began to pack the grubsack.

"Ain't you goin' to eat, Mama?"

"Time for that, after you're gone on your errand."

"But we ain't had time to talk about the parade and ever'thin'."

She hesitated a moment, then poured herself a cup of coffee and came to the table. She sat down. "How was it?" she asked. "How's Russell?"

"Fit as a fiddle, Mama. Got a landlady that looks after him."

"That a fact?"

"Seems she has marriageable daughters, so she takes special care of the bachelors."

He didn't see the look that passed over Lucy's face. He gulped coffee and dug into his breakfast.

"I declare, Little John. You're never goin' to learn to eat like decent folk. Can't you ever just take time to eat a meal proper-like?" Then, before he could defend himself, she blurted out, "Are they pretty?"

He stared at her, fork poised in the air. "What?" he asked, confusion registering on his face.

"The marriageable daughters. Are they pretty?"

"Pretty enough, but Russell, he don't aim to marry. Least-ways not one of them."

"He told you that?"

"Yes'm. Mama, did I tell you Casey come?"

"Casey? Well now, that musta been quite a surprise! Is he lookin' well?"

Little John bobbed his head up and down in response to both her observation and her question, and went on with his hurried report. "And Casey says George Brean's poorly. He's gettin' too feeble to travel."

"Likely so, Son," she replied. "He was always so strong—and such a good man. But people get old. And when they do, they can't do ever'thin' they could do when they was young." She looked sad. "Sometimes they wait too long. Person ought never to wait too long to do the things that are important to him."

Puzzled, Little John could neither understand what his mama was saying nor who she was saying it to. For some reason, it reminded him of Uncle Russell standing at the bridge talking about "giving up too soon."

"Mama," he asked, "do you reckon Uncle Russell ever give up too soon on anything?" She looked at him quizzically and he added, "What I mean is, Papa always said Uncle Russell could do anythin' he put his mind to, even if he don't have but one good arm. But one night at the bridge, he said somethin' strange 'bout how people hadn't oughta give up even when it seems like there's no use to try. Seemed like he was talkin' 'bout himself—like he was worried 'bout some-thin'. You've known him a long time, Mama. Do you think he ever give up too quick?"

She stared into her coffee cup. Finally, without looking up, she said, "Maybe one time he did, Son. Maybe he did." She stood up then and left him alone.

Somewhat bewildered by her statement, he gobbled down the rest of his breakfast. Rushing to the loft once more, he went directly to the end of the bedstead and lifted the tick.

The wheatsack was gone.

In desperation he ran his hand underneath, searching for it, knowing all the while it was not there. He stood there, heart pounding, trying to decide what to do.

"Is this what you're lookin' for?" Mama's voice startled him, for he had not heard her on the stairs. Her face was grim and in her hands she held the wheatsack.

"What call you got to go snoopin' in my room?" he demanded angrily.

"What call you got talkin' to your mama that way?" she retorted.

He hung his head, ashamed instantly of his rudeness. "I'm sorry, Mama. I can explain."

"Suppose you begin by tellin' me where you got this?" She wagged the sack in front of him.

He stared at her, seeing the hurt and anger in her eyes. He searched for what to say, knowing that he could not yet talk to her about Mitchell Callaway. "I'm sorry, Mama. I can't tell you that," he mumbled. "Leastways not just yet."

She stood for a moment then, as if debating her next move. Suddenly she threw the sack on the bed. "All right then. Take it. If you won't tell me where you got it, I don't want to hear any fancy explanations about why it was under your bedtick. Get it outta my sight and don't ever insult your mama by usin' stolen money to buy for her. I'd rather starve."

"Mama!" he protested. "I can explain, truly . . . "

But she had turned away. He could hear her stifled sob as she stumbled down the stairs.

Helplessly, he looked at the wheatsack. In that moment he knew he hated Mitchell Callaway. The anger he felt was even greater than the hate he acknowledged. Anger at Mitch for not being the man that he had made him to be, anger at Mama for not giving him a chance to explain, and even anger at Uncle Russell for not being there when he needed him.

He jerked the wheatsack up from the bed and thrust it inside his shirt. He jammed his broadbrim hat on his head and in a flash saw Mitch's handsome face beneath a hat just like this one. At once he tore the hat from his head, threw it on the bed, and hurried downstairs.

In the kitchen, his grubsack lay on the table. He reached for it and hurried toward the door. Spying an empty sugar sack on the shelf nearby, he grabbed it and stuck it inside his shirt also, knowing it would come in handy for what he had to do. Then he stomped out the door.

Outside, he met Arial coming from the barn, milk pail in hand. "I been takin' care of the milkin' while you was gone," she explained. Her eyes lit on his grubsack. "You goin' somewhere again?"

"Got business in Potosi," he said. "Be back as soon as I can."

"It's gonna be hot, Little John. Hadn't you oughta wear your hat?"

"I hope to die if I ever wear that hat again!" he yelled at her. "I'll take my chances without it." He dashed up the hill and left her staring at him with gaping mouth.

———

He rode furiously the first few miles, urging the aging horse faster and faster. At length, his reasoning overtook his

133

anger and with some reluctance he allowed that he had no call to take it out on Tony.

All the excitement of the past few days had soured in his memory now. He was home again, with responsibilities and Mama yelling at him and Arial's haunted eyes reminding him of Mitchell Callaway.

"Nobody's ever what you want them to be," he complained to the air. "Uncle Russell said Mama would understand!" He shook his head in disgust. "She won't even listen . . . what does Uncle Russell know anyway? Way off in the big city goin' to his fancy office ever' day . . . all the time talkin' 'bout helpin' out and never here when I need him . . ."

At once, a hint of guilt invaded his railing and he reluctantly admitted to himself that Uncle Russell had done more than his share of taking care of them. "Well, he ought to," he reasoned aloud. "We been takin' care of his farm all these years." Again his conscience argued with him until he allowed that Uncle Russell probably didn't want the farm, that he only kept it so they would all be taken care of.

Stubbornly he clung to his accusations that everyone had let him down. Mama, Russell, Casey, even the Brooms—he hadn't heard from Bertie since Jake and Anna Marie married—and especially Mitch. Mitch had been lying to him all the time. His thoughts tumbled over each other and his anger took control once again. Jabbing Tony with his heel, he yelled, "Giddyap!" and raced down the road.

Hours later, in Potosi, he stopped at the stable to water the horse and wipe him down. The old man in charge chewed on a piece of straw thoughtfully as he watched Little John.

"None of my business, young feller," he said at length, "but it's never a good idea to be racin' a horse in weather like this."

The sight of his horse all in a lather told Little John that the man was right; he could hardly argue the point. Still, he affected an air of indifference.

"Horse that age mebbe could die, you know," the man commented.

Little John spat on the ground. "So it dies. Horses die. People die . . . or go away. That's the way things are, old man."

"You raised up 'thout no manners, was you? Mind you, you treat people like you been treatin' that there horse, ain't no wonder they go away."

Although exasperated, Little John said nothing more until he had finished rubbing down the horse. Then, turning to the old man, he asked, "Where would I likely find the sheriff?"

Eyeing him curiously, the old man told him where to go and then suggested, "Just tie your horse there. He'll be fine 'til you get back. Mebbe even give him a chance to rest up."

"I'm obliged to you," Little John said. He fingered the sack through his shirt as he turned and walked a few paces. Looking around carefully to make sure no one would see him, he withdrew the sugar sack first and then quickly stuffed the wheatsack into it as he pulled it out. He was pleased that he could get it all in. *At least the sheriff won't see this wheatsack first off,* he thought. He pondered once more just how he would explain his errand to the sheriff.

———

Once inside the office, he found a man seated at the desk. "Are you the sheriff?" he inquired.

135

"He's gone for the day. You just missed him. Something I can do for you, young feller?"

Pausing to consider what to do next, Little John chewed on his lip.

"Got a problem?" the man asked.

"No, sir." He handed the sugar sack to the man. "Can you put this in a safe place for the sheriff?"

"Why certainly," the man assured him. "Any message?"

"Message?"

"What had I oughta tell him about this sack?"

Little John shrugged. "Don't rightly know. Just tell him I found it one day in the north part of the county."

"And who are you that found it? You got a name?" The man dipped a pen in the inkwell and poised it, ready to write down the name.

But Little John was already out the door. He forced himself to walk slowly back to the stable, mount carefully, and ride very casually away from the town.

He breathed easier once he had left the town behind. *At least that problem's taken care of.* He made up his mind to write Russell in time to post it with the next mail coach. He would tell him that he had taken care of the matter. He would also tell him that Mama hadn't listened at all . . . that she was very angry with him. Maybe he'd even tell him to sell the farm, that he didn't want to be beholden to him any longer.

The thought came to him that he could just keep on riding and never have to face Mama's anger or Arial's grieving again. He savored it for a moment before discarding the idea. "I don't aim to be another Mitchell Callaway, deserting my family," he muttered to himself, patting the horse's neck all the while. Then, to the horse, "I been hard on you for no call."

The horse flicked his ear and whinnied shortly. Amused, Little John added, "We'll take it easy going home."

Although it was long after bedtime when he arrived home, he took special care of his horse that night, rubbing him down, seeing that he had water and feed. Satisfied that Tony was well cared for, he staggered down the hill wearily, went directly to his room, and fell into bed.

———————

In the months that followed, Little John busied himself from dawn to bedtime. He avoided Mama and Arial as much as possible, saying very little but making it a point to speak politely. Partly he avoided them because he was still too angry to talk to Mama about Mitch, but partly because he couldn't bear to look at either one of them. Mama became more lost in her own thoughts every day. It seemed she was always watching Arial—when Arial wasn't looking. As for Arial, she was skinny as a scarecrow and not a bit more talkative than one.

One night, early in September, he wrote to Uncle Russell asking him if he'd sell the farm. He reasoned that Mama could always go back to the hilltop cabin. Beyond that, he gave no thought to how she might feel about his suggestion, nor what they would do if Russell did sell out. He only knew that he wanted to be done with it all. Without a word to Mama, he mailed the letter on the next coach out.

The next week the grasshoppers came. Overnight they ate away every inch of crops he had raised, and overnight Little John realized that never would he want to live anywhere but right where he was. Only now it was too late.

As sure as the sun sets over Solomon's Ridge, he conjectured, *these grasshoppers is a judgment from God Almighty.*

The Almighty's teachin' me a lesson. He's punishin' me for bein' so ungrateful and for tellin' Uncle Russell to get rid of this place.

The thought came to him as he walked the devastated fields one morning. It stayed with him through the day and then haunted him in the night. And for weeks thereafter Little John Chidester walked about sober and unsmiling, pondering in his heart the terrible thing that he had done.

CHAPTER THIRTEEN

A Great Black Cloud

ll of Dogwood Creek gathered together at the school-house and implored the Almighty to look down with mercy on them. When Arial Callaway came with her mama and Little John, the neighbors sucked in their breath at the sight of her but said not a word about her errant husband.

They returned each week—the Chidesters and their neighbors—taking comfort in one another's company, and pleading their cause before the only One who could control the grasshoppers.

Little John always sat in the back of the room, shoulders slumped and head hanging as he silently pleaded with God Almighty to overlook his past railings and give him another chance with the farm.

As the weeks passed by, the St. Louis papers carried stories from hundreds of miles away about grasshopper devastation. Little John's guilt over bringing the infliction to the community lessened somewhat when he saw that Dogwood Creek had not been singled out as the special recipient of the plague. Gradually he came to question whether the Almighty would choose to destroy the whole country over the rash raving of one person. Perhaps, after all, there was no connection. He brooded less, but deep down—in his worst moments—the question of blame still nagged at him.

But Little John's daily struggle against the grasshoppers did take his mind off Mitchell Callaway and helped to ease the tension between him and the two women. In a quiet moment with Lucy one evening he told her that he had taken the wheatsack to the sheriff in Potosi. "I didn't have nothin' to do with stealin' that money, Mama," he declared. But he did not volunteer where he had found it, and she did not ask.

They did not speak of the matter again.

———

When the grasshoppers left, there was not a farm on Dogwood Creek that had any crops to lay away. At Carrick's Mill the men gathered in little bunches and discussed whether they could make do with what was in their cellars until next crop.

Christmas came and went. Russell sent food gifts by the mail coach but he did not visit the family this year. His letter, sent on the same coach, made no mention of Little John's question about selling the farm.

As the end of January came near, Arial grew quieter day by day.

"It's the season," Lucy observed to Little John. "A year come and gone this month and not a word from that husband of hers. Seems like she's tryin' to get away from ever'thin'. . . do you take notice how she wraps herself in that shawl these mornin's? I recollect how she used to throw it on and scurry away fast as she could step. Nowadays, she stands behind the cookstove, starin' into the air, and folds that shawl around her like she's wrappin' herself into a cocoon. I reckon it's her way of shuttin' out ever'thin' that's happened."

Little John allowed that only mamas would take notice of the way a woman drags on her shawl, but still he had to agree that Arial stayed by herself more and more and it worried him.

He had little time to linger over Arial's problems however, for when the snows melted the grasshoppers returned in a great black cloud. Like other farmers, Little John tried to drive the insects away. He ran into the midst of the field, flapping tow sacks all the while. He poured kerosene diluted with water on the ground where they buried their eggs. He looked longingly at posters at Carrick's Mill that advertised the newly invented hoppercatchers guaranteed to rid farms of the plague. He joined the neighbors in their efforts as they dug ditches two feet wide and two feet deep in the path of the grasshoppers. When the insects fell into the ditch and could not get out, he speculated with his neighbors that they had stopped the great advance.

The success of the ditches greatly encouraged Little John and he began to hope that, just perhaps, the Almighty had looked with favor on him and was giving him that second chance for which he had so fervently prayed.

Then one morning, as he sat eating his breakfast, he heard a roar that brought his heart to his throat. Running out the back door he saw a cloud of grasshoppers descending over everything. He ran to the field to check on the recently dug ditch. For as far as he could see, the army of insects was coming—from the south field to the orchard, they covered everything that grew.

Dejectedly, he returned to the kitchen to tell Lucy what he had seen. "The ditches don't do no good when they're so many," he explained. "The line must be a mile wide this mornin.' Don't reckon there's any hope of farmin' this year, Mama."

The grasshoppers ate every tender shoot in the fields and stripped the orchard bare. One day, when there was nothing left to eat but the onions in Lucy's garden, they devoured those and then, at last, flew away with the wind.

Day after day, Little John sat hunched over like a little old man, talking to Mama of the devastation. What did it matter now that they had gone away? They had eaten everything in sight before they left.

"Looks like the few that stayed behind are eatin' each other now," he said bitterly, not even looking at Lucy. "Too bad they wouldn't do that to begin with."

He stared at his calloused hands, open before him on the table, searching his mind for that one more thing he might have done.

Sighing, he asked, "Do you think Uncle Russell will sell out? Don't seem like we can go on puttin' in crops to feed grasshoppers . . ." When she didn't answer at once, he added, "Likely he'll sell and we'll be done worryin' over it."

Lucy studied Little John's face carefully before she responded. "Would you like that, Little John? Would you like to be done with farmin'?"

He hung his head in his hands as he struggled for control. "Maybe the Almighty won't let me do what I want, Mama . . . " he burst out. His breath came in little jerks as he rehearsed all the fears of the past months. He blurted out everything—how he had written to Uncle Russell asking him to sell the farm, how he had at first been convinced that the plague was his fault, how now more than anything he just wanted to farm on Dogwood Creek for the rest of his life.

She looked at him, a half smile playing about her mouth. "Well, Little John," she replied matter-of-factly, "likely you're thinkin' straight part of the time. It don't make sense to figure the Almighty would punish half of the country 'cause you was actin' ungrateful. On the other hand you're wrong about Russell. He ain't never gonna sell this farm."

Little John looked up, obvious skepticism written on his face.

She eyed him curiously. "You truly are worried about that, Son!" It was an exclamation, not a question. She spoke it as though for the first time she understood the depth of his concern. "If that's all you're worried about, you can put your mind to ease," she assured him. "Russell won't sell this farm . . . fact is, you can't sell what don't belong to you."

He sat up straight at her revelation. "Don't belong . . . this farm don't belong to Uncle Russell?"

She shook her head in affirmation and he waited for her to explain.

"It belongs to all of us . . . it's the family's until . . . " She paused.

"Until what?" He urged her to go on.

"For now, it belongs to the family and we'll not be sellin' it . . . at least not yet." With that she rose and walked away, leaving him to determine the exact meaning of her words.

He puzzled about it most of the afternoon, and in the end only concluded that both he and Mama had secrets to keep.

———

In the twilight the three of them sat on the porch, catching the cooler air. Little John strained to read the newspaper in the vanishing light. It felt good to sit and read to Mama as he had done in the past—before she had found the wheatsack in his room. But when his eyes ran down the page and came to rest on a short item about the James brothers, he ignored it. Until he was ready to tell Mama the whole truth about the wheatsack, he couldn't risk reading to her anything that would prompt a discussion about Mitchell Callaway. Instead he chose an item about a grasshopper "tea" held among St. Louis society where guests were served grasshopper soup, fried grasshoppers, baked grasshoppers and something called "grasshopper à la John the Baptist."

"I reckon that means grasshoppers with honey," Lucy said, recalling the Bible story of John the Baptist. Even Arial chuckled over the idea of people serving insects at a fancy gathering. And Lucy declared, "I can't believe people'd eat 'em—ain't even fit for chicken feed."

Little John folded the newspaper and they sat then, watching the lightning bugs and listening to the nightsounds— each one lost in private thoughts—until it was time to go to bed.

———

Fall was coming on when Russell sent word that relief trains from the east were expected in St. Louis to distribute food supplies and new seed for replanting. *"I will see to it that a quantity gets to Dogwood Creek,"* he wrote. *"Expect me on Saturday in a week. Give out the word at Carrick's Mill that we will distribute the supplies at the schoolhouse on that same evening."*

Little John read the letter to Lucy and readily agreed when she said, "God Almighty has seen fit to spare the people of this community from starvation."

"And just in time," he added. "Last week, Old Man Carrick said the officials at the statehouse was pushing for all the farmers that have suffered from the plague to get together and share with one another what they have. Carrick says that if we was to do that here, there still wouldn't be enough food to last ten days."

The next day Logan Bennett stopped by as he was going to Carrick's Mill and Little John told him what Russell had written. "Mighty good of him to look after all of us," Logan said. "I'll pass the word at the mill."

When Logan returned on his way home, he brought a message from the men who had gathered at the mill that morning. "They want you to play your fiddle at the schoolhouse, Little John. Carrick, he suggested it . . . said it would help the people forget their troubles. All the men agreed right off." Plainly, Logan was enthused about the possibility of the thing the men had decided. "You'll do it, won't you, Little John?"

Little John was reluctant, declaring he would have to "practice up a lot before the doin's. On the other hand," he admitted, "I got nothin' better to do. Grasshoppers seen to that."

Russell arrived on the stage on Saturday morning as he had promised, bringing seed, as well as barrels of flour, cornmeal, beans, and dried apples. Old Man Carrick loaded it all directly onto his wagon and promised to bring it to the schoolhouse that evening.

Russell walked the three miles to the cabin and found both Lucy and Little John in the house. "Arial's up at her place today," Little John explained after greeting his uncle. "She goes there a lot these days."

Lucy had killed the last of their chickens and made dumplings. "Hope it's fit to eat," she said apologetically. "Chickens pecked on grasshoppers so long they got bound up. Some died . . . some wouldn't do to eat."

"It looks fine, Lucy." Russell assured her. His eyes swept around the nearly empty table and, almost as though he were thinking aloud, he said, "I had no idea . . . "

Lucy seemed not to hear—seemed, in fact to be in an almost festive mood. "It's been awhile, Russell," she said. "We're glad to see you."

———————

When they had eaten all that was provided, Little John took Russell to the hilltop orchard to point out the devastation. "I tried whitewashing the trunks. It stopped them for a little while—can't get their footing on the trunks. But, as you can see, it didn't stop them for long."

Russell stood there, shaking his head. "I've been worried about all of you, Son. Your mama tells me you still have some canned fruits and vegetables in the cellar. The relief provisions will help and I'll see that you make it through the winter all right. Then plant your new crop and pray. That's all you can do. . . . Little John, I hate to be adding to your troubles, but I've got something you ought to see." He withdrew a worn newspaper clipping from his pocket. "I just happened onto this at the office one day. Somebody brought it in. It's from the Independence paper. I checked afterward and couldn't find any notice of it in the St. Louis paper, so I thought you likely wouldn't see it."

Little John took the paper and read aloud, beginning with the caption.

New James Gang Member Identified
It has been learned by this reporter that a previously unidentified member of the James gang is a cousin of the Younger brothers. Bearing a strong resemblance to Bob Younger, this handsome young man goes by the name Mitchell Callaway. While this is thought to be an alias, no information on his real name is available. It is widely believed that Callaway lived in the Liberty area at one time and in more recent years, when not on the road, has lived in a remote area of Washington County. His whereabouts for the past year is a matter of speculation. Frequent sightings from widely separate places have been reported. A reward of $2,000 is set for Callaway as for other members of the James gang.

"So it's really true," Little John said flatly. "Why didn't you send this? Or leastways write me about it?"

"It was something I thought would be better said than written. A letter's kind of cold sometimes."

"I reckon you're right. You think we had oughta show this to Arial?"

"Much as it grieves me to do so, that's exactly what I think we should do."

They walked over the ridge field toward the hilltop cabin. As Arial's barn came into view, Little John was reminded of the wheatsack. "I finally told Mama what I did with the sack, but I ain't told either one of 'em that I found it in Arial's barn. After she sees that newspaper piece, guess it won't matter no more."

At the cabin, they spied Arial standing at the door. "She's skinny as a rail," Russell said in a low voice.

147

"Last year or so's been mighty hard on her, worryin' over Mitch and seein' us lose all the crops to the grasshoppers and all. Seems like she's all the time cryin'."

Arial walked slowly toward them. She hugged her uncle. Then standing back, she brushed back her hair with her hand and blinked her eyes several times.

"Arial," Russell spoke half jokingly, "looks like I'm just in time with supplies. A little more and the wind would blow you away."

"I'm glad to see you, Uncle Russell, supplies or no. And I 'spect it would take more than a wind to blow me away."

They sat on the steps in sight of the little creek. Little John was the first to speak. "Want to walk home with us, Arial? And you're comin' to the schoolhouse later, ain't you?"

"I was fixin' to come over directly," she answered. "Did you come just to fetch me? I told Mama I'd be along."

Russell crushed his hat with his good hand. He scuffed his shoes back and forth into the dirt at the bottom of the steps. Arial watched him for a minute; then, turning to her brother, she asked, "What is it? You and Uncle Russell got somethin' to tell me?"

Without looking at her, Little John answered abruptly, "It's about Mitch, Arial. Uncle Russell has something to show you."

Russell withdrew the clipping once again and handed it to her. Both he and Little John stared at the ground as Arial read the worn news clipping.

When she was finished, she handed it back to Russell. Tears rolled down her cheeks. She sobbed into her apron while the men awkwardly looked around. At length Russell put his arm around her and squeezed her, but he said nothing.

Arial dried her eyes on her apron and, looking at first one then the other, said, "I reckon I knew it all along."

"You knew he was an outlaw?" Little John suppressed a gasp.

"Oh, not when we married. But almost from the first afterwards. There was so many secrets. I started to put things together after the St. Genevieve robbery—and when he disappeared after the Gads Hill train robbery, I just knew that had to be the explanation. Only thing is, I've never once heard from him in nearly two years, so I been thinkin' he was dead. But now this newspaper . . . how long you had it?"

"A month or more."

"So he musta been alive then," Arial said thoughtfully. "Leastways this writer thought he was. But with a reward like that on his head . . . well, if he ain't dead yet, he soon will be . . . I'm so ashamed, Uncle Russell. I never shoulda married him."

"But you didn't know then what you know now, did you?"

"Oh no. But I knew you didn't think we should get married and . . . "

"Arial, as your dead papa's brother, I'm likely to have an opinion. But you were old enough to make your own decision."

"Even if it was wrong?"

"Well, looking back now, it's easy to say it was wrong, but if you didn't know at the time, it was an honest mistake, Arial. And you loved the man . . . "

"I loved a robber, a common thief . . . "

"The important thing is that you're not a robber or a common thief."

They left then, the three of them, walking mostly in silence until they came to the big cabin. In the kitchen they met Lucy and Arial burst into tears, throwing her arms around her mama. In a few minutes she regained her composure and began to explain to the puzzled Lucy what she had learned.

———————

The two men slipped quietly out the back door and walked toward the barn. When they came to the haunted oak, Russell plopped down beneath it. In an instant Little John was beside him. He had waited so long for this chance to talk to his uncle; now he hardly knew where to begin.

"I'm afraid for Arial—now that she knows the truth," he said hesitantly.

Russell raised his eyebrows briefly, questioning his nephew's meaning.

Little John went on. "She'll get like me if she's not careful." He spat out the words now. "I hated him when I finally admitted the truth. I hated him so much I couldn't think of nothin' else. I couldn't talk to Mama, I couldn't stand the sight of Arial. I needed Mitch so bad—needed him to be what I imagined him to be. I couldn't stand knowin' the truth. Knowin' he was no good, havin' to admit he had never been the friend I had thought him to be—that was the worst. I got angry at all of you all over again—you and Casey and even Papa."

He shook his head, remembering. "I felt like if ever'body else had stayed with me, I wouldn't have needed Mitch so bad." He picked up a rock and threw it down the hill.

Russell looked at him sympathetically. "You been holding all that in for a long time, Son. I can see how you feel like you've got no one to turn to. Everybody needs someone who'll not be leaving."

"Seems like I been lookin' all my life . . . "

"You've been looking for people—depending on people. First you depended on your papa to come home again, like he did after the war, then you depended on me to come to Dogwood Creek and . . . well, no matter. You depended on me and on Casey. But none of us could be what you wanted us to be, Son. People let you down, even when they don't want to.

"You remember what Mr. Eads said about the bridge over a year ago? He said a lot of times it was just him and that bridge, that nobody believed in what he was doing and he was all alone, but he always knew that the bridge would be finished. Everybody thought he should have been relieved because it passed the test with fourteen locomotives, but Mr. Eads didn't have any need to test it for himself. He knew the bridge wouldn't let him down.

"I've thought a lot about that, Little John. It's mighty important to have a bridge across the Mississippi and I'm proud to have had a part in it. But it's a lot more important to have a bridge to the Almighty and we have that, too. The Book tells us Jesus Christ was put to death on a cross so he could be our bridge to the Almighty. If you believe that and if you tell him that, it says you'll find that bridge to heaven.

"I've never been one to talk much about my religion, but it's always troubled me that there's no preacher on Dogwood Creek. There's just so much a man can do for himself and there's not a man living who doesn't need the Almighty. I think right now you need him about as much as anybody."

Little John listened carefully, absorbed in a side of his uncle that he had never seen. He waited, hoping for him to continue.

"There's something else, Little John. No matter how mad you get at Mitchell Callaway, you're never going to change him into what you want him to be. But being angry at him is going to change you—likely change you into the kind of person you don't want to be."

Little John hung his head. Russell had put into words what he had been thinking about for a long time. But he wasn't sure just what to do about it.

"When I was younger I had enough anger for three men." Russell's declaration surprised his nephew.

"I've never seen you angry in my whole life," Little John protested.

His uncle chuckled. "Like I said. There's not a man living who doesn't need the help of the Almighty. Maybe it's time for you to go to your loft and have a long talk with Him."

But Little John didn't wait to go to his loft. Under the great oak, he settled the matter once and for all. When they rose, he knew that Uncle Russell had once showed him one of the finest bridges ever built, and now he had helped him cross the most important bridge he would ever cross.

CHAPTER FOURTEEN

Papa's Fiddle

F or supper, they made do with clabbered milk and corn bread made without eggs. Lucy spread out the sparse provisions early, explaining, "No need to have to rush gettin' ready for the doin's at the schoolhouse."

When they had finished, Russell recalled that Old Man Carrick had told him Little John was to play his fiddle tonight. "Is that true?" he asked his nephew.

Embarrassed, Little John nodded. "I'm goin' to try. Got to warm up a little 'fore we go. I don't s'pose you have your French harp with you?"

"Just so happens I do," the older man replied, patting his pocket.

They pushed away from the table, moving their chairs into a corner. While Little John went to get his fiddle, Russell began a lively rendition of "Turkey in the Straw." Little John joined in halfway through the tune.

Lucy and Arial clapped in appreciation as the tune ended. Arial sat at the table, already cleared from the meal. Lucy got up and walked toward the parlor.

"You had enough already, Mama?" Little John teased.

"Just keep playin'," she replied. "I'll be back directly."

On returning, she stood quietly waiting for them to finish her favorite, "Old Aunt Sally, There's a Bug on Me."

When Little John looked up from his playing, he saw that she had Papa's fiddle case in her hand. She held it out to him. He wondered at the tears welling up in her eyes.

"This fiddle's been in your grandma MaryAnn's family for a long time—since before the first Brean come to America. I expect that you've earned the right to play it."

He looked at her in disbelief. "You mean it, Mama?" He took the case and held it almost reverently. "Papa always guarded this so careful. I'm almost afraid he wouldn't want me to . . . are you sure it's all right?"

She dabbed her apron at her eyes. "I'm thinkin' the fiddle should be yours now . . . that is, if Russell agrees. It's his family's fiddle."

Little John's eyes widened as he looked at his uncle.

"You've earned it, Son," Russell said. "Your papa would be proud."

Little John took the fiddle from the case and turned it back and forth in his hands. "I remember Papa talking about this fiddle like it was the most important thing he owned . . . how Grandma MaryAnn's brother, his uncle George, gave it to him when they left Indiana. He even told me how Grandma's great-grandfather Brean brought it from Ireland and how everywhere the fiddle went, the picture that hangs over the mantel went with it."

"That's right, Son, and don't be forgetting that. Someday you will have to give up the fiddle or take the painting, too." A smile played about Russell's lips as he teased his nephew. He laughed at his own jesting and everyone joined in.

A look passed between Russell and Lucy. It was ever so brief, but Little John saw it and wondered at the meaning.

———————

When they arrived at the schoolhouse, they found the yard already full of wagons. Inside, Little John looked over the crowded room. It seemed that everyone on Dogwood Creek was there. The thought of playing for such a crowd made his stomach hurt. Frantically, he wondered if he might find some escape. The thought had only crossed his mind when he spied Old Man Carrick coming towards him. That could mean only one thing—it was time for the fiddling to begin.

But it was Russell who Carrick came for. In his panic, Little John had forgotten all about his uncle who stood beside him at the doorway.

Carrick's voice boomed above the noisy crowd. "Mighty fine turnout, Russell, would you say? And you're the cause of it all. Ever'body wantin' to see you . . . to thank you. Whyn't you come with me?" He turned to Little John then, smiling at the sight of the fiddle in his hand. "Mighty nice of you to help us out, Son. You can start your music anytime you're a mind to."

They left him standing there. He felt a sudden relief, knowing that the attention of the crowd was all on his uncle—the man who had made the gathering possible. He made his way through the room to the platform at the front. Hoping no one was looking, he seated himself, took the fiddle from its case, and tucked it under his chin. After a few tentative swipes with the bow, he began.

He sat up straight as a young sapling as he played "Soldier's Joy." The sound of Papa's fiddle took his mind off the crowd. Hearing the clear mellow tones, his mind was stirred with memories of his childhood when they lived in the hilltop cabin and Papa played almost every evening.

Halfway through his third selection, he was distracted by a young couple coming through the door. It was his sister, Anna Marie, and her husband, Jake Broom. Little John almost lost his timing when he saw the auburn-haired young woman walking with them. There could be little doubt—it was Bertie Broom, all grown up.

The three were making their way toward the platform and by the time the piece ended, Anna Marie was standing almost at Little John's elbow. She threw her arms around his neck. "I declare, Little John, your music puts me in mind of Papa. You are a mighty fine fiddler."

Holding the fiddle at arm's length to protect it, he kissed his sister on the cheek. "You're a sight for sore eyes. I'm glad to see you!" He nodded to Jake. "I'd shake your hand, but I got none to spare right now." He laughed, clearly pleased to see Jake.

Anna Marie looked closer at the fiddle and declared, "I thought that sounded like Papa's fiddle. How long you been playin' that?"

"Tonight." He laughed. "This is my very first try." Turning to Jake again he asked, "What brings you here?"

Before he could answer, Anna Marie said, "He'll explain later. First we got to say hello to Mama. Where is she?"

Little John pointed to where Mama sat and they walked away, leaving him staring into the face of Bertie Broom.

He was still staring when Russell coughed at his side. He bowed slightly to Bertie and said, "I just came to check on why the music stopped. I can see there's a reasonable explanation." He looked at Little John's reddening face and

156

back again at Bertie. "Please forgive my nephew for staring," he said with exaggerated concern, "but then you have grown into a beautiful young woman."

Scarlet-faced, Little John stammered, "Hello, Bertie."

She laughed. "Hello, Little John."

She waited for him to speak. Again it was Russell who broke the awkward silence. "I saw your brother and Anna Marie across the room. What brings you all back to Dogwood? Can we get some seed for you? Or maybe some flour?"

"I reckon not, Mr. Chidester, thank you. My pa is getting some relief supplies down New Madrid way. We heard 'bout the doin's and come over to see you all. Jake's taken a job at the mines over yonder hill near Potosi and I hired on at the rooming house where we're all stayin'. We figured it was time we done somethin' to help, what with the grasshoppers and all."

Little John found his voice. "So you're livin' between here and Potosi?"

She nodded, tossing her long curls over her shoulder. "I don't s'pose you ever get over that way?"

"Never can tell . . ."

Uncle Russell broke in very seriously. "Little John is likely to have business down Potosi way any day now. Right now, you'd better play us another tune, Son."

Reluctantly, Little John raised the fiddle and ran the bow across the strings a couple of times. Then, turning to Bertie, he asked, "Would you have a favorite you'd like to hear?"

Her green eyes sparkled as she replied, "I recollect one your papa used to play—said he'd never heard anyone outside your family play it."

Little John grinned. "The Grand Picnic." He tucked the fiddle under his chin, tested the bow once more, and began to play. He shut out everything else and concentrated on the tune, hearing it again as he had heard it as a child. It seemed to him that he had never played so easily. He bore down on the bow, raising the volume of the fiddle, until the sounds of the ancient instrument filled the schoolhouse. When he had finished, every eye in the room had turned to him. The people clapped wildly and the young men whooped their appreciation.

Embarrassed at the attention, Little John nodded his acknowledgment and murmured something about sitting out a spell. Carefully he placed his fiddle in the case and went to join Bertie who still stood nearby. With his hand under her elbow, he guided her to where his mama sat visiting with the girls and Jake.

Bertie hugged Mama but said nothing to Arial who sat next to her until Arial moved forward and said, "Hello Bertie."

"Oh Arial!" Bertie exclaimed. "I didn't know you . . . you're so . . . that is, you've changed." She hugged Arial then, saying, "It's good to see you. I hope we'll be seein' more of the Chidesters now that we're back in these parts."

Arial smiled at her and hugged her tightly, but before she could respond, Anna Marie mumbled, "You'll be seein' more of one of the Chidesters, that's for certain." She looked at Little John.

"Bertie," Little John said, pretending to ignore his sister's remark, "could we find a seat over there and you can tell me what's been happening since I saw you last?"

"I can tell you that, Little John," Anna Marie volunteered. "She's been growing up."

Bertie blushed.

Ignoring the laughter of the others, the two of them made their way to some benches not too far distant.

Once seated, it was Bertie who spoke first. "Little John, I didn't even know Arial. She looks so peaked . . . Is it 'cause of that outlaw she married?"

His mouth fell open and, for a moment, he could find no words. Then he asked, "How did you know 'bout that?"

"Pa gets the paper from Independence now and then. Saw a piece 'bout Mitchell Callaway being a member of the James and Younger gang."

"Lately?"

"No, a month or more ago."

"Musta been the same paper that Uncle Russell has. We just seen it for the first time today. We ain't heard from Mitch in almost two years."

"What does your mama think, Little John?"

"Hard to say. She just heard today. But I reckon Mama's suspected it for a long time. For that matter, so has Arial."

He stared off almost as if he had forgotten she was there. "Arial'd be the first to tell you she made an awful mistake marryin' Mitch, but none of us think she's got cause to be ashamed now. She never did nothin' wrong."

So lost were they in conversation that they didn't hear Cassie Miller approach them. They looked up in surprise when she blurted out, "As I live and breathe! Bertie Broom! It's been a long while since I laid eyes on the likes of you. You comin' back here to marry Little John, are you? You was always sweet on each other."

Little John eyed her evenly. The woman had always annoyed him somehow. "We was both little kids when Bertie moved away, Cassie. I reckon you always had some kind of imagination."

Bertie seemed not the least flustered by Cassie's boldness. "We've moved to the Big Mine area between here and Potosi,

Mrs. Miller—me, and Junior and Anna Marie. Junior—Jake we call him now—is workin' in the mine. I found me a job at the roomin' house where we're all livin'."

Before Cassie could speak further, Little John stood up, hand beneath Bertie's elbow, urging her to stand also. "We got to go now, Cassie," he said abruptly and walked away. "Nosey old biddy!" he said, when they were far enough away not to be heard.

"She's just an old woman, Little John. She don't mean no harm." Bertie seemed pleased at his embarrassment.

"Old is right. And she's spent her life pokin' into other folks' affairs."

"Oh, I don't know," Bertie replied. "I've seen worse."

"Worse than Cassie Miller? Now that I'd like to see. She's the talk of Dogwood Creek, has been for years."

She turned to him then, lifting her chin saucily. Her face broke into a grin as she asked, "Did you ever stop to think that sometimes she may be right?"

He felt his heart skip a beat. He caught his breath, wondering how to ask her to explain what she meant.

Once again, his uncle interrupted. "There you are! I'm sorry to tear you away, but we do need you to play one more piece. Logan Bennett and Old Man Carrick will be giving out the provisions soon as you're through. Figured that another tune would help get some order before we begin . . . and by the way, that was mighty fine fiddling, Little John . . . sounded just like your papa."

Normally seeing the pride in his uncle's eyes would have been all the encouragement Little John needed. But, right now, he had more important things on his mind. "But Bertie and me . . . " he tried to protest.

"I'll take care of Bertie," Russell assured him. "It's just one more tune and then you're done." He tucked his good hand under Bertie's elbow and guided her away through the crowd.

Little John dared not look for them as he played "Speed the Plow." The ease with which he had played "The Grand Picnic" was now gone. He concentrated on every note, determined that when he was finished, he would spend the rest of the evening with Bertie.

As the last note of the fiddle died away, Old Man Carrick mounted the platform. Raising his hands to signal quiet, he asked the group to bow their heads with him as he thanked the Almighty for the provisions they were about to distribute. Little John glanced over the room, hoping to locate Bertie, but saw only that men everywhere were doffing their hats and bowing their heads. He didn't even have time to put away the fiddle before bowing his own.

Carrick was thorough in his prayer, thanking the Almighty for the provisions; for the people in the East who had sent them; for Russell Chidester who had seen to it that it was brought to Dogwood Creek; and even for Little John Chidester who had brought so much pleasure tonight with his music.

Little John squirmed during the prayer and as soon as the "Amen" was said, put his fiddle away, took up the case, and went directly to where Mama and Arial sat. He looked from one end of the room to the other, but Bertie was nowhere to be seen.

"They left, Little John," Arial volunteered.

His heart sank. "Left . . . already?"

"They got a long ride back to Big Mine." She spoke almost apologetically, as if she understood his disappointment.

"But Bertie . . . Anna Marie . . . none of them even said good-bye."

"Yes they did," she replied. "They told me to tell you 'good-bye.' And Bertie, she even said, 'Tell Little John we're staying at Ellison's boarding house in Big Mine.' "

He lay awake a long time that night, recounting all that had happened from the time Uncle Russell arrived that morning. Listening to his uncle's heavy breathing from the cot next to him, he wondered how one day could hold so much sadness and so much happiness all together.

"Thank you, Almighty God," he prayed in the darkness. "First for makin' it all right between me and you . . . and for the provisions . . . and if that wasn't enough for one day, you brought Bertie . . ."

He chuckled thinking about that. "I don't know for sure if the Almighty brought her or not, but I'll thank him anyway." He closed his eyes then and conjured up the image of Bertie Broom walking by his side and saying that Cassie Miller might have been telling the truth.

CHAPTER FIFTEEN

Outlaw at Dogwood Creek

———————— ∿ ————————

The next morning, Little John awakened to the sound of Mama's broom pounding on the ceiling below his loft.

Seeing that the sun was already up, he jumped out of bed and dressed hurriedly.

In the kitchen below, he found Lucy, Russell, and Arial sitting at the table, evidence of their already eaten breakfast before them. Mumbling something about the chores, he hurried to the back door.

"Never mind, Son," Lucy said. "Russell did them for you."

Little John looked chagrined. "I'm sorry. Why didn't you wake me, Mama?"

"I wouldn't let her," Russell volunteered. "I figured if a strapping young man like you didn't wake up with the roosters, that you might need some extra sleep."

"You're forgettin' there's no rooster to wake up to." Little John smiled halfheartedly as he spoke and sat down beside his mama.

Ignoring the reference to their dire circumstances, Lucy said, "You did your papa proud last night, Son. Fine fiddlin'. Fine party."

"Thank you, Mama." He warmed under the compliment. "It was a great party—except for Cassie Miller."

The women looked at him quizzically, but Russell burst into laughter. "That woman's been the fly in the ointment for all the Chidesters since we first came to Dogwood Creek. Why should it be any different for you?" Still chuckling, he added, "Bertie explained to me what happened."

"Maybe one of you could explain to me and Mama," Arial suggested, "or is it some big secret?"

"With Cassie Miller around? A body ain't likely to have a secret for long." Little John pretended indifference.

When he offered no information, Russell quickly volunteered the details. "Cassie said to Bertie—right in front of Little John—'I reckon you come back to marry Little John Chidester.' " For the next five minutes he filled them in on his nephew's embarrassing incident of the night before.

Little John's face reddened, but he laughed with the rest when the story was over. As the laughter died down, he found himself thinking about Bertie and searching for words to tell Mama how he felt.

His thoughts were interrupted by the scraping of a chair as Russell rose and, looking at Arial, announced, "I'll fill the water bucket one more time before I leave to catch the stage. Want to walk along? I have something to discuss with you."

The door had hardly closed behind them when Lucy lay a hand on Little John's arm. Smiling softly, she said, "Russell told me about your talk under the haunted oak . . . I hope you don't mind."

He shook his head thoughtfully. There was so much he wanted to say to Mama—about Bertie, about Uncle Russell, about the Almighty.

"He's been good to us, hasn't he?" he asked, his eyes searching Mama's.

"Hard to tell if you're meanin' the Almighty or your Uncle Russell, Son, but I reckon it fits both of 'em."

He laughed lightly at her and then fidgeted.

"Somethin' on your mind?" She asked the question gently, with no hint of prying.

He flashed a great smile at her and blurted out, "Mama, I'm goin' to marry Bertie Broom!"

To his surprise, she didn't even raise an eyebrow. "Does Bertie know about this?" she asked.

"Well no, not yet." Seeing the smile on her face, he exclaimed, "You're teasin' me."

She laughed shortly. "I am at that."

He waited, knowing that she would tell him what she truly thought.

"I'm not surprised, I'll say that first off. I got eyes, Son, and I saw you lookin' at her last night. And if you're wonderin', do I approve, I reckon you know how I've always felt about Bertie . . . like she was one of my own. You'll never find a finer woman . . . but Little John, you ain't hardly old enough to take on a wife."

A look of horror crossed his face. "Oh Mama, I don't intend on marrying her tomorrow or even next month. But . . . maybe . . . "

She waited for him to find the right words.

"I was thinkin' maybe after my birthday next year, after I'm eighteen. Gives me more than a year to get things in shape here . . . and to convince Bertie to marry me."

"That part don't worry me none. Gettin' things in shape here is a different matter." She looked distant as she continued, "Would be nice to think it could all be in shape by your eighteenth birthday."

"I been thinkin' 'bout that." Little John talked all in a rush now as if he couldn't wait to get it all out. "I could work in the mines and buy provisions to keep us until next year's harvest."

"How would you expect to have a harvest, if you're off workin' the mines?"

"I don't know, Mama . . . " He frowned.

"You have some big decisions ahead of you, Son, and you been doin' a man's job for so long it's hardly fittin' for me to tell you what to do anymore, but I wish you'd forget about the mines. If the hoppers don't come back, you'll have plenty of work to do here."

"What if they do come back?"

"We can talk about that when the time comes."

Russell coughed at the doorway. "I couldn't help hearing . . . "

Little John looked at his uncle standing there, and it came to him that Uncle Russell had been giving him advice for more years than his own papa had—and he had always given good advice.

"What do you think, Uncle Russell?" he asked.

"Your mama's right . . . unless, of course, you really want to quit farming and work the mines the rest of your life."

Little John shook his head emphatically. He had settled that question once and for all. If he had a choice, he would never leave the farm.

"Then let me carry things until you know for sure about next year's crops. Then we can . . . " He cleared his throat and began again. "That is, *you* can decide about what to do after that." Glancing at Arial who stood near the wash stand, he added, "I'm trying to convince Arial to come to St. Louis. I'm sure my landlady would have work for her and she'd be safe living in the same rooming house where I live."

Little John and Lucy looked at Arial, their eyes widening in surprise.

"You goin' today, Arial?" Little John asked.

"I can't. I got to think on it awhile. I don't ever look for Mitch to come back, but still I can't make up my mind to up and leave just like that. I feel like ever'thin' is just hangin' and I can't hardly make any decision until it's settled some-way or another."

"If you change your mind, write me and I'll send stage fare," Russell urged. He left then, reminding all of them that he would send supplies regularly on the stage.

———————

Winter came early to Dogwood Creek. The first snow fell suddenly and piled deep. The creek froze over for a mile or more. In the cabins scattered along its banks, the people hovered by their heating stoves and speculated on whether or not the freeze would be deep enough to kill off any eggs the hoppers might have left.

On sunny days the men would plow their way through the snow to Carrick's Mill. There they passed the time, sitting around Old Man Carrick's stove, talking about the last hard winter—the winter that William John Chidester died. They argued about the exact year, some saying it was '57 and some '58. Old Man Carrick settled the matter by reminding them that William John died of the fever in January of the same

year that his namesake, Little John, was born in December—
and that was 1858.

They recalled then how they had buried William John at
the schoolhouse and how the seasons had come and gone and
how the graveyard that started with him now held a couple
dozen graves, including four Chidesters.

Invariably this point brought them to the latest discussion
of the Chidester family: the question of Mitchell Callaway—
hadn't they known from the first that he was no good?

Had they not all been convinced that Callaway had treated
Arial Chidester scornfully, had they not all been full of praise
for the Chidester family, they would not have felt so free to
talk in front of the Carricks. After all, Carrick's nephew had
married the middle Chidester girl. But since with one voice
they proclaimed Mitchell Callaway a scoundrel who had
brought shame to a good family, they talked freely—unless,
of course, Little John happened on the scene.

Their discussions brought them each time to the
unanswerable—indeed the unthinkable—question: "Where
would the outlaw be buried?" Not that anyone thought for a
moment that Callaway would ever show his face around
Dogwood Creek again. Still, it was an interesting question
to ponder. If perchance he came back, and if perchance
someone was to put a bullet through him for the reward
money, how might the body be disposed of? Surely not in the
schoolyard next to decent folk. But if not there, then where?
Their conjecturing always ended at that point with Carrick
himself proclaiming, "No use talking about it. Mitch Callaway ain't never goin' to show his face around these parts
again." More often than not he added, "I reckon I'm to blame
for Arial's troubles. If I hadn't up and given the man a job he

wouldn't have stayed around long enough to marry one of our girls."

————————

The Chidesters avoided Carrick's Mill that winter, depending on Logan Bennett to bring the mail and the supplies that Russell sent. While Arial was glad to stay away from prying eyes, Little John grew restless over the long months.

He had made two visits to see Bertie before the winter set in. Now he had to content himself with rereading the two letters Logan had carried to him from the mill—and with memories of their last visit.

They had ridden double on his horse and taken a picnic supper after she was finished working at the rooming house. It was well after dark when he had brought her back, reluctant to start his long ride home. Coming to the hitching post, they had sat for a moment savoring the coolness of the evening and the great moon overhead. "That's what they call a harvest moon, I reckon," Little John had said. "Only there's nothin' to harvest under it this year."

"Do you recollect when we was kids, how our families made molasses under the harvest moon?" Bertie had asked. Her arms had still circled his waist as when they were riding.

With one hand he had held the reins, and with the other he had covered her hands. "I 'member," he had said quietly. "It was a happy time." He had mumbled something then about the next time there was sorghum to cook, they would make molasses again under a harvest moon. It had been an awkward attempt to say something to her about what he was feeling, only it didn't come out right.

Disgusted with himself, he had climbed down then and tethered the horse. He had held his hand for her to step into and she had slid gracefully down. They had stood there, his arms about her waist, her eyes bright under the moonlight. "Is that a promise, Little John?" she had asked, a smile teasing about her mouth. "Will you truly bring me to a molasses making?"

His arms had tightened about her waist. "That's a promise." He had buried his face in her hair and thought to himself, *And there are more promises to come*. He had wanted to settle the matter then, had wanted to speak of other promises, but he could not bring himself to make promises he might not keep—not until he knew what the future held for him could he talk about what it held for the two of them. Instead, he had lifted her face to him and kissed her lightly on the lips. Her arms had held him close, responding to his embrace.

He had forced himself not to say another word, not even to tell her that he loved her. For that in itself would have promised something. Reluctantly he had reached for her hands and, holding them in his own, had said, "Bertie, there's so much I want to say. But now ain't the time. I can't help but think about Mitchell Callaway and all the promises he made to Arial—to all of us in one way or another—and how he broke ever' last one."

"Little John," she had protested, "You're nothin' like Mitchell Callaway."

"No, I'm not like him. If I broke promises, it would be for different reasons than he had. But, all the same, I vow I'll never be like that, makin' promises I can't or won't keep."

He had left then, thinking that she understood.

Now he wasn't so sure. Through the long winter months there had been only the two letters, both of them cool and impersonal, filled with news about what they were doing, but not once mentioning anything about harvest moons or future visits.

———————

When the snows melted, there was no sign of the hoppers. As the season of plowing began, all of Dogwood Creek began to hope that the insects were gone for good.

Late one afternoon, after a long day of plowing, Little John came into the cabin whistling "The Grand Picnic." After supper he brought out Papa's fiddle and played the tune again, remembering the night that Bertie had come back into his life. After putting the fiddle away carefully, he went to find Mama, hoping that she was alone.

He found her sitting in the kitchen, darning in the pale evening light. He sat down beside her, wondering how he should begin. "Talk is that the hoppers are gone for good, Mama."

She nodded. "I hear that's the way most folks look at it."

"Likely we'll have good crops this year."

Again she nodded.

"Maybe we'll have things in order by the time my birthday comes in December."

"Little John, do you have somethin' on your mind?" She let her darning fall to her lap and looked up at him.

"I aim to ask Bertie to marry me," he blurted out. "Soon as plowin's over, I'm fixin' to ride over there and settle it." The words were hardly out of his mouth when a call at the back door interrupted them.

Logan Bennett stood on the step, lantern in hand. "Evenin', Little John," he said. "Evenin', Lucy." He touched his hat brim as he greeted her.

"Logan! Do come in," she urged.

"Some other time. I need Little John to come with me . . . got something to tend to."

"I'll get my lantern," Little John replied, without questioning the neighbor. Knowing that only an urgent matter would bring Logan on an errand at night, he waited for the older man to explain.

He didn't have to wait long. As soon as they started up the hill, Logan announced bluntly, "Mitchell Callaway's back. I found him yonder in my cave, a bullet in his side."

Stunned, Little John could hardly find his voice. At last, almost in a whisper, he asked, "Is he alive?"

"Was when I left him—barely. I thought you ought to know about it . . . didn't want to tell Arial myself."

As they walked, Little John listened attentively to Logan's account of how he had found Mitch. "I was walkin' the field this morning—just daylight it was—and I spied three horses tethered at the mouth of the cave. One for sure was Callaway's mount—didn't recognize the others. I had to think on that for a spell—three horses means three men—didn't want to take on more than I could handle. So I went about my business—plowed the ridge field outta sight of the cave. No chance to see anything else, and when I come back after supper the horses were all gone. First off, I thought, 'Well that's that. Whoever was here has up and gone.' But I was curious about what mighta gone on in the cave so I went home to get my lantern. When I come back, that's when I found Mitchell Callaway."

They were standing at the mouth of the cave. Little John's mind was racing. In all his pondering over Mitch, he had not once imagined that they might meet again—certainly not in this way.

"I'll go first," he volunteered. He clambered down, lantern in hand.

Logan followed close behind. Once on the cavern floor, he lifted his lantern high and, jerking his head in the shadowy light, motioned to the far wall. "Over there," he said.

In a moment, Little John was squatting beside the wounded man.

"Hello, Mitch."

"Hey there, Little Buddy," Mitch whispered.

Little John felt the anger welling up at the sound of Mitch's familiar greeting. Remembering Uncle Russell's warning, he prayed silently that Almighty God would keep his anger from coming back and swallowing him up again.

Logan had found a canteen of water laying nearby and he handed it over. "Perhaps he'd like a drink."

Little John held Mitch's head up and pressed the canteen to his lips.

"Thanks, Little Buddy." Then, his breath rasping, Mitch asked, "Did you find the money . . . the money I left for Arial?"

"I found it all right . . . " Little John was about to tell Mitch that he had taken the money back to Potosi without Arial ever knowing about it, but Mitch interrupted.

"That's good," he said and closed his eyes.

Logan squatted beside them now and leaned over Mitch. "Callaway, s'pose you tell me what you're doing in my cave anyway."

"Come back to see Arial," Mitch explained. Two friends came along. Almost made it . . . someone fired at us about a half hour down the road . . . the governor's put a price on my head." He paused. "I was the only one that got hit . . . we came here . . . hid out for the night . . . friends . . . they left this morning early. Said they'd feed my horse before they left . . . "

"Your horse?" Logan posed the question.

"You see him tied outside?"

"I saw him this morning," Logan volunteered. "But he's gone now, Callaway. Maybe your friends needed an extra mount."

"They wouldn't do that . . . " Mitch struggled for breath.

"Well they did do it. I reckon men such as them don't think much about takin' a good horse when they see one. You oughta know, you been ridin' with them outlaws ever since you come to Dogwood Creek."

"They're good men, Bennett."

"Good men don't rob banks and trains."

"They're just avenging themselves . . . jayhawkers made things hard for them during the war."

"War's been over nearly ten years, Callaway. How long can a man use that for an excuse?"

Mitch lifted his hand feebly toward Little John, moaning with the movement. "Here, L.J." he began. He lowered his hand again and pushed at something beside him. "Take this . . . for Arial. Tell her I came back."

In the shadows Little John could make out a wheatsack, knotted in the middle. He heard the clink of coins as Mitch pushed it toward him. Angrily he exclaimed, "No, I won't!" His voice echoed on the cavern walls. Struggling to control himself, he spoke more quietly. "You asked did I find the sack—the one you left in the barn—and I told you I did. But you didn't wait for me to tell you what I did with it." He enunciated each word now as he looked at the dying man. "I took it to the sheriff in Potosi and that's exactly what I'll do with this."

"You had no right . . . That was for Arial."

"Arial don't need you to steal for her. Me and Uncle Russell, we been takin' care of her."

"That's a good buddy, now take . . . "

"You can quit callin' me 'good buddy,' Mitch. Good buddies don't steal from each other. I know about the hides . . . you even stole from your own brother-in-law and I was just a kid!"

Mitch lay very still. In the lantern light, Little John could see his lips moving. He leaned over him, ear to Mitch's lips. "What did you say?" he asked.

"A man's gotta do what he has to do . . . " Mitch whispered the words slowly and closed his eyes.

In a moment he was gone.

CHAPTER SIXTEEN

A Shroud in the Cave

When Little John came in from milking the next morning, Arial was standing at the cookstove, stirring the gravy. He studied her face and tried to recall what she had looked like before all her troubles began. It puzzled him how a woman could age so over a man.

At least her troubles are over, he observed. *She won't have to worry about him no more. Now, if I can just find a way to tell her that her outlaw husband is dead . . .*

"Mornin', Arial," he said, then looking at Mama who was taking up the biscuits, "Mornin', Mama."

"Mornin', Son," Lucy replied.

Arial went on with her stirring, making no acknowledgment of the greeting.

Little John stood near the table, his eyes fixed on his sister. *Just my luck,* he thought. *She's in one of her ponderin' spells—likely she don't even know I'm here.* He sighed deeply, causing Lucy to look at him.

"Somethin' wrong, Son?"

He knew she must be curious about his late-night errand with Logan, but she wouldn't ask him outright. He glanced at her, then at Arial, and again at Mama. "I wish Arial'd sit down 'fore she stirs a hole in the pan," he said.

At once, a look of understanding crossed Mama's face. "Arial!" she called loudly.

The younger woman looked up, startled, and waited for Lucy to say something. When she said nothing, Arial turned to Little John.

"Oh . . . hello," she said, as though seeing him for the first time that morning. "You were out kinda late last night with Mr. Bennett."

"We had something to tend to," he replied, searching for some way to begin. Crossing to the cookstove, he poured some coffee from the pot and then sat down at the table.

"I can see, you're needin' to say somethin', Son." Lucy put a plate of biscuits on the table and sat down beside him.

He studied her for a minute before replying. "Fact is, I got to talk to Arial . . . to both of you . . . but . . . " He paused, exasperated, and then spoke to his sister. "Arial, we got to talk."

She gazed at him, studying his expression, but she didn't sit down. With slow and deliberate movements, she turned back to her gravy making. From where he sat, Little John saw the set of her jaw and knew that she knew.

So why won't she sit down? he asked himself. *Why's she makin' it so hard for me?*

"Arial, can't you sit down a minute?" he asked, a hint of anger in his voice.

"No I can't. Not if you want some breakfast," she replied and stirred so hard the gravy slopped over the edge of the cast-iron pan.

"Sit down, Arial," Mama commanded, moving quickly to the younger woman's side. "I'll take this up. If you cook it any longer this gravy won't be fit for nothin' but paste. Anyway, it's plain as the nose on your face that Little John has somethin' he wants to say to you."

Arial moved slowly to the table and sat down. "Uncle Russell sent you another newspaper piece, did he?" she asked, a trifle wearily.

"No, Arial, no newspaper pieces."

"But you do have news about Mitch." It was a statement, not a question.

He reached across the table and took her hand. "Arial, Mitch is dead."

She stared woodenly at him then. "Well, I reckon it comes as no surprise." She looked past him with vacant eyes, color draining from her face and for a minute he thought, *There she goes again—likely I'll never get through this* ... At length, she turned toward him, her eyes searching his. But she said nothing.

"He died last night," Little John volunteered. "A gunshot wound."

"How'd you happen to know, Little John?" Her expression registered no more than idle curiosity over this bit of information. But it gave him the opportunity to tell her what had happened.

"Logan and me, we was with him."

"You was with Mitch . . . where?" Her full attention was on him now. "Where was he? And why didn't you take me to him?"

"He was in the Bennett cave, Arial. And I didn't know he was there until after I left here with Logan."

"Are you sayin' that Logan Bennett knew my husband was in that cave and came and fetched you and didn't tell me about it—not one little word?"

179

She jumped up from her chair as she spoke. Clearly agitated, she jerked the corner of her apron from one hand to the other.

"Don't be too hard on Logan, Arial." Little John stood up to face his sister. "He didn't know what to do. He wanted to talk to me before tellin' you. He didn't know Mitch was as bad off as he was. He thought there'd be more time."

"How much time does a body need to come and tell a woman that her husband that's been gone for nearly two years is hidin' out in some cave and dyin' without her there? You shoulda fetched me."

Her voice rose in hysterical sobs and she pounded her fists against Little John's chest. "He was an outlaw and he was no good. But he was my husband and I loved him more'n life itself. I shoulda been there . . . I shoulda been . . . " She ran from the room sobbing into her apron.

Little John moved as if to follow, but Lucy grabbed him by the arm. "I'll go," she said. "I'll give her a few minutes, then I'll go."

He sat down again, slumping in despair.

Lucy sat beside him. "Don't brood over it, Son. You done what you thought best. A body can't always know . . . " She passed food to him, silently urging him to eat his breakfast.

He spread two biscuits on his plate, covered them with gravy, peppered the whole until it was nearly black, and began to pick at it absentmindedly.

"We have to make some decisions, Mama. Logan will be by directly. We have to know what Arial wants to do about the body." He stared off into the room and spoke slowly and emphatically. "Personally, I think she should turn it in and collect the reward money."

"Little John!" Mama scolded. "I'll not have you speakin' that way. God Almighty knows your sister's been through enough. She don't need her family a-sayin' anythin' to remind her what kind of a man Mitchell Callaway was."

Little John didn't look up. "I know that, Mama. All the same, I hate what's happened to her. I've watched Arial turn into an old woman. I declare she looks like she's the mother in the family and you're the older sister."

"Another time I might appreciate the flattery, but right now I'm sorry for Arial. She's had more'n enough trials to make her look old. We got to figure how to help her, Son. She can't go on like her life's over 'fore it hardly started."

" 'Course you're right, Mama. But likely things won't be no easier now. Once Cassie Miller gets ahold of all this, ever' tongue on the creek will be waggin'."

"Likely so, Son. On the other hand, Cassie Miller's always held that the James gang is a bunch of brave men that was done wrong and they are to be admired. Not likely that she'd fault Mitch for his outlawin'. Still it won't be easy for Arial to hafta listen to tongues waggin' whether they're for or against her dead outlaw husband."

She rose then and went after her daughter.

———

By the time they returned, Little John had eaten his breakfast and thought of a plan. He waited for the women to eat before he spoke. "We'd best talk 'bout arrangements," he declared.

Arial looked at him directly, but said nothing.

"Logan's coming by any minute, Arial. Before he does, I have an idea." Seeing her waiting for him to continue, he began. "We have a problem 'bout burying Mitch, do you understand that?"

"I know it's not the same as burying our pa." Her voice was sharp as she answered him.

He determined to make her understand. "Arial, Mitch has a price on his head, dead or alive. Now it's not likely anyone on Dogwood Creek would bother the grave, but if word gets out . . . well, we can't tell but what somebody might come and dig up the body."

"To claim the reward you mean?" Her eyes widened with sudden understanding.

He nodded. "I'm sorry, Arial. We have to think what could happen."

"Oh my! That would be unthinkable." Her eyes darted from Little John to Lucy and back again. "But what on earth can we do?"

"Only one thing I can think of, and that depends on Logan."

"Logan?"

"I think we might bury Mitch where he died. In Logan's cave. 'Course we'd have to go with a shroud instead of a coffin. Havin' a coffin made would mean more people would know . . . word's bound to get out."

Arial listened intently. The expression on her face told him that she was pleased with his plan even before she spoke.

She scraped back her chair, went to his side, and put her arms around his neck. Kissing him lightly on the cheek, she said, "Thank you, Little John. I'd like that . . . to do it exactly as you said . . . if Mr. Bennett will allow it."

She examined the gold band on her finger thoughtfully. "There's something else . . . if we bury him in the cave, I can say my good-byes private like . . . I'd be obliged to Mr. Bennett—and to you—for that."

She tried to make amends then for her earlier outburst but he waved it aside saying, "No need for that, Arial. I can't rightly imagine all you've been through. You got call to go a little crazy now and again."

A knock at the door announced Logan Bennett and he was quick to see the wisdom of Little John's plan. "If you have somethin' for a shroud, we can take care of ever'thing by afternoon," he said.

Lucy left the room at once and returned with a quilt. "Perhaps this would do," she suggested, handing it to Logan.

But Arial reached for it, saying, "No, not this one. If Little John don't mind, he could fetch the one from my bed at the hilltop cabin . . . the one you gave me when we was married, Mama. I want to bury him in that."

That settled, Logan suggested that Lucy should ride over to fetch Cora to sew the shroud. He and Little John walked along with her to the barn and saddled Tony. When she had gone, Little John found a pick and two shovels for digging the grave. Logan took the tools and went on to the cave, while Little John went to the hilltop cabin in search of the quilt.

Alone in the room where Arial and Mitch had slept, he studied the intricate pattern of the quilt. Mama had once said it was a "Double Wedding Ring." He had been just a boy when Mama had made the quilt for Arial's wedding. *She's made one for all the girls,* he remembered. Suddenly his mind went to Bertie—was it only yesterday he had told Mama he was going to ride over to Big Mine and ask Bertie to marry him?

He ran his rough workworn fingers across the quilt wondering what Mama must be thinking now. Somehow it seemed a sad ending for the quilt. He folded it into a small bundle, tucked it under his arm, and hurried away to Bennett's cave.

————————

It was midafternoon when Arial arrived at the cave. Carefully she picked her way down the rungs, coming to a halt at the bottom. Little John waited for her to get accustomed to the semidarkness. He could see that she had put on her good dress and brushed her hair back neatly. She had tied it at the nape of her neck the way Mitch always liked it.

"Mama offered to come," Arial volunteered. "But I told her there was no need."

Little John nodded in understanding and guided his sister to the far side of the room. "He's over here, Arial."

Cora Bennett sat to one side of the shroud, her sewing notions in a small tin box nearby. "Hello, child," she said kindly. "I'm sorry about your troubles. Logan told me you was comin' so I waited to finish sewing the top of the shroud until after . . ."

"I'm obliged to you, Cora," Arial said. She stifled a sob as she looked at the form, encased in the quilt up to the neck. A large flap of the quilt lay under the head, sufficient to completely cover when the time came.

She moved quickly to where the body lay. She sat down in a position where she could lift Mitch's head onto her lap. "Mitch, Mitch," she cried, shaking her head all the while.

Little John sat in silence with the Bennetts, watching as his sister whispered over and over to her lifeless husband. Except for the rhythmic plopping of water onto the stalagmites, there was no other sound. The cool, dank air filling his nostrils seemed suddenly oppressive. He wondered if he would ever forget the smell of it or the sound of whispering mingled with dripping water.

At length, he went to Arial's side. "We'd best get on with it, if it's all right with you."

Carefullly, she placed Mitch's head on the ground once more, and leaned over to kiss the cold forehead. Turning to look at her brother, she said, "No man ever brought so much happiness and so much pain to the same woman as he did. I wished for so long that things would be different . . . finally I just gave up. But now, seein' him here, I remember how much I loved him . . . but I loved a man that never really was and I'm cryin' over losin' what I never really had."

She reached for Little John's hand and he helped her up. Then she turned to Cora and said. "I'm obliged to you, Cora. You and Logan—you're such good neighbors."

She wiped her eyes on her apron and went to stand at the foot of the ladder where she could see the daylight overhead. Little John moved to her side and stood with her while Cora finished her work.

In a short while Cora came, her tin in hand. "I'll stay with her, Son," she said. "I'm all done now."

Together, Little John and Logan heaved the body into the grave. For a brief moment, the cavern sounded of their heavy breathing, and then it echoed from the shovels scraping moist earth over the shroud. When it was over, the stillness seemed greater than all the echoes before. Once again Little John was conscious of the dripping sounds.

With the shovels stilled, Arial turned, searching for the faces of the men. Logan looked at her sympathetically and said, "We're done here . . . Mrs. Callaway."

She walked to the shallow grave, stooped over and patted the dirt down at the head. "Good-bye, Mitch," she whispered.

"I thank you, Mr. Bennett," she said, rising to her feet once again. She climbed carefully up the ladder and the others followed close behind.

Logan came up last and, after making sure all the tools and lanterns had been handed up, threw the ladder to the floor of the cave. Standing before Arial and Little John, he pulled Callaway's wheatsack from inside his shirt. He held it before them, a question on his face.

Little John started to explain about the sack to Arial.

"I reckon I know what's in it," she said. "Do what has to be done with it, Little John." Her eyes pleaded with him now. "I'd be obliged to you . . . "

Logan spoke up then. "Little John, if you want, I'll see that it gets to the sheriff's office over at Potosi." He hesitated before adding, "One more thing, Arial. This cave's a secret place. Nobody on Dogwood Creek 'cept your family knows of it. I reckon it'd be hard for Mitch's friends to find their way back here. What I mean to say is, if it's all the same to you, I'd like to keep it that way."

"It's your cave, Logan," Arial answered. "What I need to know is what I can tell people 'bout Mitch."

"Ever'body already knows he was involved with the James and Younger gang, Arial," Bennett said kindly.

"That's true enough. But it don't help me to know what to say 'bout his dyin'.'"

"You don't have to say anythin', unless you want to. But if the subject comes up, tell folks he died from a gunshot wound and that he was buried where he died. Leave it go at that."

"Thank you, Logan . . . Cora." Arial hugged the older woman and then the Bennetts left.

Little John carried the tools and Arial swung the unlit lantern in one hand as they walked in silence over the ridge.

After a time, he said quietly, "I had my own problems with Mitch, Arial, but Uncle Russell helped me see what I could do about them." Fumbling for the right words, for he was not accustomed to giving his older sister advice, he encouraged her to trust God Almighty to help her forget about what was past and to begin thinking of the future.

She listened attentively, not seeming to notice his discomfort. "Time was when I did the worryin' over you, Little John. Now seems like all of a sudden you've grown up . . . taken on all the worries of the family." She caught his arm with her free hand. "You've grown to a fine young man, Little John," she said, a look of admiration on her face.

She gave him no time to respond, but talked on of what she might do. "I been thinkin' of somethin' Uncle Russell said. You 'member he asked if I wanted to come to St. Louis to live?"

He nodded.

"Do you think it could be the right thing for me to do now?"

Little John stopped still and looked at her. Her eyes were red with crying, but he fancied that some of the pain was gone from them. "If it will bring back our old Arial, I'd be for it. All the same, I'll miss you." He noticed her eyes brimming again.

Abruptly she began to walk again. As he fell in beside her, she teased, "You won't have time to miss me—you'll be runnin' your horse to death back and forth between here and Big Mine." She laughed lightly and sniffled.

"Have you talked to Mama about goin' away, Arial?"

"No. I aim to do that as soon as we get to the cabin."

———

Lucy quickly approved of Arial's plans, adding, as Little John had, that she would miss Arial.

"You'll not lack company for long, Mama," Arial said. "One day soon Little John will marry Bertie Broom and he'll fetch her to the hilltop cabin." Her voice caught. "It'll be a happier place when he does . . . and you'll have 'em for company."

"No," Lucy said, seeming not to notice Arial's emotion. "When Little John marries, I'll go back to the hilltop cabin. He'll live here."

"You won't!" they both protested.

"I will," she said emphatically.

"Because Papa built it?" Arial asked.

Lucy searched their faces carefully as if memorizing every feature. "Partly . . . but there are other reasons. I've studied on it a good spell." With no further explanation she concluded, "A body can't always know what the future holds . . . but it's good that we never stop dreamin' about what's around the corner."

CHAPTER SEVENTEEN

The Legacy

❧

hree weeks later, Lucy sat alone in the parlor gazing out the window. In her lap lay a waist of Arial's—the last to be mended for her move to St. Louis.

She pondered over the fact that, for the first time in all her forty years, she would be alone soon, and it gave her both pleasure and a feeling of sadness. She was happy for her children—Russell was coming for Arial today and Little John was going this very night to see Bertie—but she felt a bit melancholy over her own prospects for the coming years.

If only . . .

Her thoughts were interrupted as Little John came into the room. He stooped to kiss her on the cheek. "I'm goin', Mama. Tell Uncle Russell I'm sorry I hafta run off 'fore he gets here. But I'll see you all in the morning."

She looked at him approvingly. His thick raven hair was parted high on one side and fell forward over half of his forehead. Blue-black eyes sparkled at her from beneath dark bushy brows. His finely chiseled jaws, browned from working in the fields, framed a full, well-formed mouth that was parted in a smile at this moment. He had spent a long morning in the fields, but ever since dinner, he had been getting himself ready for his ride to Big Mine. He had taken a basin of water to his loft room and she heard him splashing around for half an hour or more. Just as the clock struck two, the splashing stopped and the whistling began. It was now nearly three and she allowed that the time had been well spent.

"You're a right handsome sight, Son," she said. Her eyes shone like his at the thought that tonight Little John would ask Bertie to be his wife. It was on her lips to give him the usual cautions about minding his manners, but somehow it didn't seem fitting for the occasion. Instead she grabbed his hand, squeezed it between her own, and said, "I'll be anxious to hear about ever'thin' in the mornin'."

————

She didn't see him until breakfast the next morning, for he slipped out to do the milking while she dressed in her bedroom. She took special pains with her hair and put on a clean apron over her best calico dress. By the time she came to the kitchen, Arial had started the breakfast preparations and Russell was sitting at the table fingering a steaming cup of coffee. She sat down beside him just as Little John came in from the barn. After shaking his uncle's hand, he joined them at the table.

At Lucy's request, Russell said a prayer of thanks for the food, and for the Almighty's special keeping.

"Long night, was it?" Russell asked as he dipped a portion from the bowl of hot mush.

"Short night, long ride," Little John replied.

"From the looks of that grin, I'd say you didn't mind it none," Arial said.

Little John glanced around the table, meeting each one's eyes in turn and grinning all the while. Finally, turning to Lucy, he announced, "Bertie's goin' to marry me."

"You don't mean it!" Lucy feigned surprise. Everyone laughed as she concluded, "I'm pleased for you, Son—'specially since you told me almost a year ago that you was going to marry her . . . what I mean is, it's good that you agree on it!"

There was a babble of congratulations and then Russell asked, "When's the big day?"

"We ain't decided for certain. But I'll be eighteen in December—Bertie figured it would be a good way to celebrate my birthday . . . me, I've never liked birthdays, leastways not my own."

The room grew silent.

"I can understand that, Little John," Arial said sympathetically. "With Papa dyin' on your birthday and all—well, I know it's always been hard for you." She looked thoughtful for a moment, before agreeing, "Maybe it's a good idea to get married on that day . . . maybe it would help you have a better feelin' about it."

Before he could respond, Lucy spoke up. "No, Little John. You can't do that."

A look passed between her and Russell before she concluded, "Any day but that. You can't get married on your eighteenth birthday."

He searched her face for some explanation. She in turn stared steadfastly at Russell and he at her.

Looking mystified, Little John said, "Mama, it's not that important to me and Bertie don't care, but . . . "

"Then that settles it," Lucy said abruptly. "I need you to be here on that day. And if you'll do that for your mama, it'll likely be the last thing I ask of you."

Still puzzled, Little John said that of course he would be there on that day, and for the whole week after, that they could be married a week later just as well. He even suggested that he could make a point to be with her every year on that day if it was that hard for her.

"No need for that, Son," she answered him hastily. "This ain't for me . . . it's for . . . well, no matter—just be here."

Little John looked at Uncle Russell then, as if searching for some explanation, but Russell turned his attention to his bowl and ate heartily of his breakfast.

By the time breakfast was over, the mood had lightened considerably and the talk had turned to Arial's new job waiting for her in the city.

"She'll be working for my landlady, Lucy, and living in the same building," Russell told her, "so she'll be safe enough. I'll keep an eye out for her."

"That the same landlady who has the marriageable daughters?" Little John asked.

"The very same. Only it's daughter. One of them married."

"I expect she's still takin' good care of you then—that is, as long as she has one daughter left," Little John boldly teased his uncle.

"Uncle Russell, you're blushin'," Arial joined in.

Russell looked at Lucy helplessly.

She shrugged. "Sorry, Russell. They're shameless and without manners." She said it lightly, but there was an edge in her voice when she added, "Maybe you'd like to tell us about this landlady's daughter. You fixin' to marry her, are you?"

Exasperated, Russell questioned Little John. "Why did you bring this up after all this time? Don't you remember what I told you about those women?"

"Matter of fact I 'member exactly what you said."

Lucy looked up expectantly, as Little John paused.

"So tell the womenfolk, will you?" Russell encouraged him.

"You said that if you ever did marry, it would not be one of them."

"Well, I'm glad to see your memory's accurate," Russell said. "Now can we forget about the landlady's daughters?"

Little John was still chuckling when Russell turned to Lucy. He lay his hand on hers and said, "Perhaps you'll come to see Arial in St. Louis?"

Her eyes widened in surprise. "Why I'd like that, Russell—if it'd be no trouble."

It seemed to her that Russell was surprised then, as if he had not expected her to answer as she had.

He stood up, scraping his chair back and grasped his useless arm. "I'll take my last walk to the springhouse," he said.

Lucy followed his movement as he massaged the limb that hung loose in his sleeve. Her eyes met his and in a moment she made a decision. "I'll go along with you," she offered.

As the door closed behind them, Arial took up the dishes from the table. "Do you have any idea what's goin' on with Mama?" she asked Little John.

"No, Arial. I was just thinkin' I hope Bertie is easier to understand."

He spoke of it to Russell that night as they prepared for bed in the loft. "Sometimes I don't understand Mama at all," he said.

"What don't you understand?" Russell asked.

"Don't you think she's actin' strange?"

"No, Son, I can't say I've noticed."

"Well, take today. She's been laughing all day for no reason. And she was all the time kinda teasin' ever'body—mostly you—I can't hardly 'member when Mama was like that."

Russell didn't really answer. He mumbled something about "Women aren't made to be understood," and rolled over on his cot.

———

They left the next day—Russell and Arial. Lucy insisted on walking with them to Carrick's Mill where they caught the stage, and Little John went along. Cassie Miller was there picking up provisions so they knew that by sundown all of Dogwood Creek would know Arial had gone to St. Louis with her uncle.

The older man shook hands with Little John firmly and said, "Mind you, I'll be out soon after your birthday, Son. Meantime, take good care of your mama here." He stooped and kissed Lucy on the cheek and then stood back while the two women embraced.

Little John and Lucy walked home in silence, enjoying the passing scenery. Coming to a papaw tree, Little John stopped and examined it for green fruit. "I'm all the time thinkin' of Grandma MaryAnn when I come to this tree," he said. "When I was a little boy, I come here in the wagon with her once and we stopped. Musta been later in the season . . . I picked some ripe papaws."

"I recollect the time," Lucy replied. "You was a little tyke. Your papa was off to the war. Hard times."

At once he regretted that he had reminded her of unpleasant things. He looked at her, an apology on his lips. But she was watching a squirrel overhead, smiling all the while. He shook his head in wonder. *Uncle Russell's right. There's no understandin' women.*

———

The season of growing passed quickly and all of Dogwood Creek allowed that their prayers had been answered: the Almighty had given them crops enough to spare. The harvest came and went and this year there was no fear of winter.

As December came near, the men gathered around Old Man Carrick's stove and conjectured on how Mitchell Callaway had died. "A gunshot wound it was, and they buried him where he died," Carrick reminded them. And each time they argued over where that might have been. Some said it was yonder near Gads Hill, some argued that it was clean over in Clay County, but Logan Bennett said not a word.

On one thing they all agreed—Cassie Miller had been right. More than a year ago she had wagged her head and proclaimed to everyone who would listen that Bertie Broom had come back to marry Little John Chidester. And now December was coming on and folks up and down the creek talked of little else but Little John's coming marriage. Of course there was still the question of where they would live to be argued. Little John himself had said that he would bring Bertie to the hilltop cabin where both he and Bertie had lived at different times as children. But it was known that Little John's mama had different ideas.

"She's bound Little John will live in the big cabin that was MaryAnn's and William John's," Carrick insisted. And all the men nodded, declaring in the end that they would just have to wait and see.

———————

On the morning of his eighteenth birthday, Little John awakened with a familiar feeling in the pit of his stomach. He looked about the loft sleeping area that had been his ever since Papa and Grandma MaryAnn died. He remembered every birthday since. As he had grown older he had come to understand this vague uneasiness that greeted him each year on this date. With the passing of time it had lessened, but it never really went away. He encouraged himself to remember that today was different—that in a week he and Bertie would be married.

Still he dressed more slowly as he always had on this day, battling the inevitable—and unreasonable—feelings. Determined to put them aside, he walked down the stairs, following the aroma of fresh coffee and frying sausage.

Mama had already laid out the table.

Looking about the provisions, he noted that, as always, a special breakfast had been prepared. Over the years it had become her custom to fix all his favorite foods, beginning with fried bread for breakfast and ending with gingerbread and vinegar sauce for supper. Somehow it never took away the birthday feeling, but he had come to appreciate her efforts.

Now that he was about to leave home, he recognized there had been a special closeness between him and his mama in all the years since Papa died—except for the problem over Mitch Callaway. It had almost—but not quite—made up for growing up without a papa.

She was humming to herself as he entered the room. She looked up at once, smiled, and motioned for him to sit down. After pouring his coffee, she went into the parlor. When she returned she had the painting of his great-great-great-grandmother Brean in her hands. Sitting down beside him, she explained, "Little John, it's only fittin' that you should have this picture painting now that you're gettin' married. It's from your papa's side of the family, you recollect, and your grandma MaryAnn wanted you to have it."

Then, turning the painting over, Lucy removed from the back of it a folded paper stuck under the frame. "And this paper's for you."

Little John examined the paper. For just a moment a forgotten fear gripped him in his stomach. "It's the paper from Grandma MaryAnn, isn't it?"

His mother nodded.

"You've kept it hidden in that picture all these years?"

Again she nodded, a smile of anticipation creeping over her face.

Little John stared past his mama for just a minute. "I was always afraid of that paper somehow. Can't exactly remember why." He laughed softly.

"Read it," his mama prompted.

Slowly, so as not to tear the faded paper, he unfolded it. It was dated the day after his birthday in the year 1868—the day after Papa died and the day before Grandma MaryAnn died, he noted silently.

Written in the labored handwriting of his dying grandmother, the note said simply that on his eighteenth birthday the farm was to pass to William John Chidester, the II.

For a moment he did not comprehend. While he recognized it as his rightful name, he had never in all his life heard anyone refer to him by that title. Confused, he looked at his mother.

She smiled at him.

He took up the note again, reading the last part aloud. " . . . will pass to William John Chidester II, the seventh child of the seventh son of the seventh child."

A long forgotten scene flashed before him. "Was that what she was tryin' to tell me? She kept talking about seventh children."

"I 'member you told me that it frightened you. Then Russell read the note to me after the buryin'."

"So he knew about this all along . . ." Little John shook his head wonderingly. "I knew he was a good man, Mama, but I never knew he was puttin' all that money into the farm just to save it for me."

Lucy nodded. "Your Uncle Russell's all the time tellin' me how your grandma was right in givin' the farm to you. He don't have any use for a farm. Never did have the same feel for the land that you have or that your papa had. But he was set on helpin' us to hold on to it 'til you was old enough to take care of it yourself. I reckon the time has come. 'Pears to me you'll do right by it."

She took the picture then and rehung it. Returning, she sat with him, eating and listening as he began to talk at once of his dreams for the farm. At length he jumped up, saying it was high time he tended to his chores.

She reminded him that Russell would be there in time for dinner and began to hum once more.

———

For the rest of the morning, Little John busied himself in the barn, mending some harness. He forgot to check the sun

198

until his stomach reminded him that it should be dinner time. He peeked outside and found that the sun was creeping past its noonday position. Quickly he put away his tools and walked out the door nearly bumping into Russell as he did so.

They shook hands eagerly, both talking at once.

"Your mama told me she gave you the paper making you the rightful owner of this farm today. But I could have seen that by your face even if she hadn't." Russell grabbed Little John in a great hug, adding almost in a whisper, "I thank Almighty God this day has come."

They drew apart, both blinking furiously. Little John looked at his uncle, his lips quivering with emotion. "I can't ever thank you enough . . . you've been mighty good to me—to us."

As if making an effort to lighten the mood, Russell slapped Little John on the shoulder. "Well now, that's not going to change. I'll be here, if you need me." They stood quietly for a moment before Russell continued, "There's something I want to ask you."

The tone in his uncle's voice caused Little John to look at him intently.

"Do you remember your first birthday after your papa died, how you asked me something right here in this barn?"

"I 'member asking you to be my papa, if that's what you mean. I couldn't forget such a thing as that. I still get red just thinkin' 'bout it."

He waited for Russell to continue. When the older man said nothing, Little John prompted him. "What did you want to ask me?"

"Suppose I told you that I thought you had a good idea way back then? Suppose I told you I still think it's a good idea?"

Little John stared at Russell. "Are you sayin' you aim to ask my mama to marry you?"

Russell grinned at him. "Suppose I told you that she thinks it's a good idea?"

"You've already asked her?" Little John's face registered surprise and then understanding. "Of course you did . . . when you was here before . . . didn't you? That's why she's been so . . . different these last few months."

"Different?"

"All the time hummin', for one thing."

"I think that's a good sign, Little John," Russell remarked and they both burst into laughter.

Still chuckling, Little John pressed his uncle for an explanation. "I'm puzzled 'bout something," he began. "You always said Mama would never leave Dogwood Creek and you would never come here to stay . . . "

"I was wrong, Son. It was my idea that she would never leave. I gave up too soon. I'm going to stay until after your wedding next week and then I'm taking your mama to St. Louis. We'll be married there."

They walked down the hill then, Russell's arm thrown over Little John's shoulder. A beaming Lucy met them at the door. "Food's not fit for fodder, if menfolk don't come to eat it in time."

Russell shook his head. "She's already scolding me."

Little John kissed his mama. "I'm glad for you and Uncle Russell."

As they were eating, Russell withdrew some money from his pocket and handed it to Little John. "I brought this to you as a wedding gift, only my thought was you might want to buy something for your bride, like a horse of her own. Won't do to ride double the rest of your life. Too hard on good horses, and yours is none too good to start with."

Little John gave a low whistle. "Seems like I got a lot to thank you for, Uncle Russell . . . we're both mighty lucky to have you." He looked at Lucy as he finished, "That right, Mama?"

She nodded and shyly reached her hand out to Russell.

When Little John had finished eating, he walked to the door, took his coat and hat from the peg, and then turned and looked at Lucy once more. They held one another's eyes, smiling all the while. "I'm glad . . . for both of you," he said again.

Whistling to himself, he walked outside and paused to look at his farm. In the stark winter landscape he could see to Solomon's Ridge and beyond. Snow had not yet come and everywhere there was a bare, grey look to things. He shivered in the crisp air as he gazed up the hill. The great haunted oak stood naked in the December sun. For a moment he imagined that he saw a big roan horse standing there and on its back sat Grandma MaryAnn, smiling and thrusting the paper toward him. He blinked and the vision was gone.

I wonder what she was like at my age. Little John pondered the thought awhile. Then, in a sudden inspiration, he made his first decision as landowner.

"I'll be late, Mama," he called through the kitchen door. "I'm goin' to look for a roan horse for my bride."

Joy Pennock Gage was born in the Missouri Ozarks. She and her husband Ken spent five years in rural mission work, two of which were in a logging camp. They have ministered together in churches in California, Oregon, and Arizona. Joy is the author of numerous books, including *Is There Life After Johnny?* and *Every Woman's Privilege.* She currently lives in San Rafael, California. Joy's father, B.F. Pennock, *is* the seventh child of the seventh son of the seventh child, and she did have a great-grandmother named MaryAnn.